In Winters Past

The Meade Lake Series, Book Three

Copyright © 2020 T.D. Colbert

Published: T.D. Colbert 2020

www.tdcolbert.com

Cover Design: T.D. Colbert

Editing: Jenn Lockwood Editing

ISBN: **eBook-** 978-1-7352169-4-2

Paperback -978-1-7352169-5-9

THE MEADE LAKE SERIES

IN WINTERS
past

T.D. COLBERT

For you, Mama. Thank you for being unconditional love personified. I adore you.

1

"Got another wedding for ya," Marge hollers to me from the back room. I zap out of the daydream I'm currently dwelling in as I stare out the window at my perfect mountain. Marge's Cakes and More has *the* perfect location—the best in Meade Lake, if you ask me. You can see Meade Mountain in all its glory, standing tall, looking down over all the beauty in its valley. I love my mountain.

"Another?" I say, pushing off the counter and walking toward the back. "When's this one?"

"Next week," she says, pulling the batch of cupcakes she's baking from the oven just before the timer begins to beep incessantly.

"Wow, short notice, huh?" I say. She nods.

"Apparently, the bride was bringing in some big cake from some hoity-toity couture cake place in D.C.," Marge says, tugging off her oven mitts. "But apparently, they cancelled on her last minute to take some senator's daughter's wedding."

"Yikes," I say. Marge smiles her big ol' cheesy grin I love so much.

Marge is a staple here in Meade Lake. Her family has been here for generations, before there even *was* a lake. Back in the twenties, a bunch of locals got together and worked with the county and state on this big project: a deluxe lake town and ski destination. A few years later, they dammed up Bluestone River, carved a hole with seventy-some miles of shoreline in the valley, and let the water flow. Boom. Meade Lake was born.

"I thought maybe you'd like to take this one," she says to me. My eyes grow wide. She grins again. Marge is a heavier-set woman with a big chest and a big heart to match. She's got black hair speckled with gray that she always ties into a long braid down her back. Mom worked here throughout my high school years—that is, when she made her shifts—and I used to love coming in with her. I became obsessed with baking and icing and cake decorating. So much so that, when I graduated, Marge offered me a job, knowing I wouldn't be leaving Meade Lake and that my mom needed all the extra financial help she could get. More than a decade later, I'm still here. But I really do love it. And I'm getting pretty damn good at it.

"Me?" I ask.

"Yes, you," she says. "It's been fourteen *years*, Jules. Fourteen years. You've been the best damn assistant I could ever ask for. But frankly, I need a break every now and then, and you're damn good at this. I know you can do it."

I tilt my head as I look at her. In some ways, Marge is the only person in the world who puts their full faith in me.

"Okay," I sigh. "Did she send in an order?"

She shakes her head.

"No. She's sending the groom to place it," Marge says with a chuckle. "Wonder how that'll go."

I smile.

"It's always dangerous when you send a man to do a woman's job," I say.

"Well, if you think you have it, he will be here soon," she says. "I'm gonna finish up these cupcakes for Annabelle's birthday tomorrow, and then I'm gonna head out."

"Let me finish those," I tell her. "You go. I'll close up after he leaves."

"You sure?" she asks. I shoot her a look.

"Marge, *go*. I'm the best damn assistant, remember?" I ask, holding my arms out. She laughs.

"Proud of you, girl," she tells me as she grabs her coat off the hook behind the door.

I walk to the back and grab the order sheet that's pinned above the big wooden table where the cupcakes are cooling. I mix icing with some blue dye until it's *just* the right hue for Annabelle's birthday party. It's a mermaid theme, so we have these adorable little sea creatures that I'm sticking inside them. I arrange them in our handy little carrying case and add in a personalized mini fish scale cake that Marge threw in as a bonus. Annabelle is the daughter of Ryder Casey, another local like me. We grew up here, a group of us, and most of us are still here. Some have scattered, but the rest of us will probably die here one day.

Some of us have already almost died here. But that's another story.

Just as my mind is about to go down a road I know

3

gets darker as it winds, I hear the bell above the door chime.

"Be right out!" I call from the back, sticking the last of the fish scales to the side of the cake then sprinkling it with edible glitter for an extra-magical effect. I clap my hands together and untie my apron as I walk around the corner to the door. But as I do, my apron catches on the handle of a fondue pot, sending it crashing to the ground. I fumble to pick it up, making even more noise as the metal bangs against the tile of the floor.

"Everything's fine!" I call back out. "Be right there!"

I quickly grab everything, dust myself off, and take a quick breath before pushing on the big swinging door.

"Sorry about that," I say, blowing at a piece of hair that's fallen from my ever-so-graceful pile of hair on the top of my head. "You must be—"

I freeze when my eyes finally land on him, standing tall and broad at the front counter. His lips curl into a grin as he looks me up and down.

"Well, goddamn, you haven't changed a *bit*, Grey," he says, holding his arms out and walking toward me. Ty Hunter, the hunky older brother of my used-to-be-best friend, Shane. I tried to sneak a peek of him changing once through the crack in his door. I was unsuccessful.

"Ty?" I ask, bewildered, because, although Ty is still pretty dreamy, I forgot how much he looks like his brother. I forgot what seeing Shane used to do to me. And I didn't realize what seeing someone who merely resembled him would *still* do to me. He reaches me and pulls me in for a long hug, and it feels surprisingly good. Like some of the simplicity of that time in our lives is back for a minute.

"You look the same," he tells me, holding me back and looking at me again. "I see you haven't gone gray yet," he says, flicking one of my auburn locks off my shoulder. I laugh and playfully pat his chest.

"Look who's talking. You're three years older, remember?" I ask him. "How have you *been? You're* the groom? Getting married, huh?" I ask. He smiles and nods, that grin on his lips again.

"Yeah, I've been busy, obviously," he says with a chuckle. "Mel is amazing, honestly. No idea how or why she chose me, but she did, so I'm trying to get her to the altar as fast as possible before she changes her mind." We laugh as I walk back behind the counter to get my notepad.

"Well, that's really amazing, Ty," I tell him. "You deserve it, seriously. Although, it's surprising that Meade Lake's most eligible bachelor isn't off the market already!"

He laughs and waves his hand.

"Oh, stop. You know that wasn't me. That was that bastard brother of mine." He laughs. Then the air between us grows cold, like the Meade Lake air. Our eyes meet, and then his drop to the counter as he awkwardly clears his throat. I should ask him about Shane, see how he's doing, what his life looks like.

But I can't.

I clear my throat and flip to a blank page.

"So, what is your fiancée looking for?" I ask him. He nervously fumbles with his phone to

pull out the gigantic, bulleted list that Mel must have given him. I stifle a laugh while I watch him scroll to the top.

"Okay, so, she wants a wooden base, with, uh, white fund- fond-..."

"Fondant," I finish for him. He smiles.

"Yeah, that. She wants it to be sort of 'rustic-y,'" he says with air quotes. "Whatever that means. We're getting married at the lodge at the resort, so she wants it to be sort of a woodsy theme, I guess." I smile and nod. We get a lot of those.

"No problem. I have a few photos of similar cakes you can send her to see if any of them are in the right direction."

I plop a giant book in front of him and flip through to the options. He snaps a few photos,

and within a moment, his phone is buzzing on the counter.

"Hey, baby," he says. I can hear her shrill voice blasting through the other side. A smile tweaks at his lips again. "Mhmm. Uh huh. Yep. She said she can do that. Jules. Jules Grey. She was Shane's best friend in high school. We all grew up together. Uh huh. Yep, I'll tell her. Okay, baby. Love you."

I shake off the mention of Shane's name and force a smile as he hangs up.

"She loves this one," he says, pointing to the second option I showed him. "She wants sunflowers, if that's doable. Oh, and she said to tell you you're a genius."

I laugh and close the book.

"Absolutely, not a problem."

I walk to the register and plug in the numbers, making sure to give them the friends-and-family discount. After all, his family used to be like my own. He hands me his card for the deposit and signs the receipt.

"This is awesome, Jules. We're so excited. It's so

good to be home," he says, putting his wallet back in his pants. I smile and nod.

"I'm happy for you, Ty. Really," I say. He pats my hand and turns toward the door.

"You'll deliver the cake day-of, right?" he asks.

"Yep, we have it down to a science," I tell him. He smiles.

"I'm sure you do. But I was asking more for Shane. He'll be wanting to see you."

I stare at his back as he makes his way out of the shop.

Ya know, Ty, I'm not so sure that's true.

2

I finish cleaning up the shop, lock up, and get out to my car, the late autumn air biting at my face.

I slam the car door shut and pull my phone out of my pocket.

"Hey," Kirby says loudly, trying to talk over the bar noise behind her. "I'm at Lou's."

"I saw Ty," I say.

"What?"

"I saw Ty," I say a little louder.

"What about a fly?"

"I saw TY!" I yell, and she gets quiet.

"Was Shane with him? Is he in Meade Lake?" she asks.

"No. But he will be."

"Get to Lou's," she says then hangs up. I almost smile. My cousin is a lot of things, but sweet is not one of them. She's quickfire, to the point, direct, and can be damn devastating if she needs to be. She's a year older than me, and we were always more like sisters than cousins. When my mom was...incapacitated...she and her mom became my other place to land.

I pull into the parking lot at Lou's Lakeside Grille a few short minutes later and walk through the big swinging door. I see my cousin, her thick black curls bouncing off her chest as she walks from table to table then back behind the bar. I smile at the sight of her. She's in her element in a bar.

I remember, back in the day, thinking of how different we were. Thinking she'd be the one to stay, but I'd be the one to get out. I'd come back to visit her, letting her live vicariously through all my stories about the wild west.

But I never left. So I'm here with her.

And it's actually been okay.

"Get over here," she calls to me, waving a dish towel at me as she fills two beer glasses. I walk toward the bar, and she points to the stool in front of her. The stool next to me slides out, and Luna, another one of our childhood friends, plops onto it. I lift an eyebrow in her direction.

"You didn't think you were gonna mention Shane and only Kirby would know about it, right?" Luna asks. I turn back to Kirby, and she shrugs her shoulders.

"Spill."

I let out a long sigh.

"Ty is getting married, here at the resort."

Luna scoffs.

"Of course he is. Fucking rich-ass Hunter kids," she mutters, taking a swig of the beer that Kirby gave her. The Willington Resort is one of Meade Lake's biggest tourist attractions, but for some of the locals, it's a bit of a sore spot. When the Willington opened when we were teenagers, a lot of the other small businesses suffered a major loss of business. With a little help, some of them have recovered, but some, like Luna's family business, hasn't quite made it over the hump yet.

"His fiancée sent him in to order their cake," I say.

"He still fine as hell?" Kirby asks. Luna shoots her a look. "Shoot me daggers with those eyes all you want to. But you *know* the one thing the Hunter brothers were not was ugly. My *god*, I never understood why you didn't tap Shane's ass while you had the chance."

Now I shoot her a look. She knows better. She holds her hands up in surrender.

"Alright, alright. So, what did he say?"

"He asked if I was going to deliver the cake the day of the wedding. Said that Shane would be excited to see me."

Luna and Kirby are speechless for a moment, and it makes me uneasy.

"Do you...do you think he will be?" Luna asks.

I shake my head.

"If the last fourteen or so years is any indication, I can't imagine he's desperately waiting to see me again."

Kirby sucks her teeth and shakes her head.

"Fuckin' prick."

Luna laughs.

I stand up and push my stool out.

"It's been more than a decade," I say, trying to keep my voice casual. "It's all water under the bridge now."

Kirby snorts and puts a hand on her hip.

"Jules, after everything that happened with you two, it ain't just water under the bridge. You know it. I know it. And Shane knows it, too."

I push my stool back in and look up at her.

"I'm headin' home," I say. They say their goodbyes, and I drive the few miles across town, up the mountain, and into the driveway of my little cabin. It ain't much, but it's mine. There's no mess, no man. No mom.

But I sit in my driveway for a moment, my head resting against my seat.

He had held me so close, that last time we were together. He'd kissed my forehead. He'd said he was sorry.

And then, he left.

THE NEXT TWO weeks fly by way faster than I am ready for. I've had this day marked on my calendar for two weeks, doing my best to ignore it as I walk by. I'm adding the finishing touches to the cake when Marge walks in, whistling as she makes her way to it.

"Damn, girl, what did I tell you?" she says, smacking the table, her eyes dancing with delight. "You're gonna run this place one day. I mean that. That is the most beautiful cake that's ever come out of this shop."

"Marge," I say. "That's not true. But thank you. I'm pretty happy with it."

Marge reaches into the cabinet next to me and pulls out her old digital camera. She snaps a few pictures and puts it back as she stands back to admire it.

"I mean it, honey. You are an artist." She squeezes my hand. "You sure you don't want me to take it?"

Bless Marge. She knows the story. She knows the history. What she *didn't* know was that the bride that called was Ty Hunter's fiancée. Otherwise, she'd never have let me take the order.

I shake my head. There's no way she can get this

thing in there by herself on a good day, let alone when her arthritis is acting up.

"Nah," I tell her. "I called the resort. I'm gonna go up early and try and sneak it in before any of the wedding party gets there. Wish me luck!"

"Good luck, honey," she says as I scoot the cake onto the rolling cart we had made especially for transport. I load it carefully into the back of the shop van, take in a long, deep breath, and drive off to the resort.

I pull up to the side entrance and put my flashers on. I hop out and knock on the door, and one of the waiters pushes it open for me and props it open. I unload the cake as carefully as ever then wheel it up the ramp and in through the doors.

The lodge is set up beautifully with string lights everywhere, the big A-frame window at the front looking out over my perfect mountain. I push the cart across the dance floor toward the cake table at the corner of the room and carefully slide it off onto it. I add the last few sunflowers and the toppers then step back to admire my work. I let the wait staff know it's all set up and turn to make a break for the exit. Mission accomplished. No sign of Shane whatsoever. Guess it just wasn't meant to be. Or maybe, it's that I'm rushing fate. But either way, I'm scot-free.

I reach for the door handle, but just as I go to push it, it opens from the other side, sending me sailing across the threshold and into a wall of a chest. Two hands steady me on either side, and I step back.

Then I freeze.

"Hi, Jules," Shane says.

THEN, FALL OF SOPHOMORE YEAR

"So, what's the plan for this weekend?" Luna asks as she drops her bag on the floor beside us and sits down across from me at the lunch table. I shrug and pop another fruit snack into my mouth. I'm a child at heart, and I'm not afraid to admit it. She rolls her eyes as she reaches across to steal one.

"We are not sitting around for the fourth weekend in a row, Grey," she says.

"Who's sitting around where?" Kirby asks, plopping down next to me with a grunt.

"Us. Your cousin here doesn't seem to want to do anything involving social interaction," Luna says, flicking her long black locks back and letting them cascade down her back. I swallow and look down at the empty wrapper in front of me. Kirby clears her throat.

She knows why I'm not up for much. She knows it's because my mom is getting worse. It's been six months since my dad left, and with each passing day, I'm watching my mom slowly but surely circle the funnel, right into the bottom of another bottle.

"Hey, you," Daniel says, creeping up on Luna from behind. Kirby and I feign barfing sounds, and he kisses her neck and dramatically spins her to him for a full-blown makeout session. They're so...gross.

Luna's been with Daniel for a few months now, and it's not really a secret why. She may as well be on the cover of a magazine, and he's one of the best corner-backs in the county. Add in his classic, Ken-doll good looks, and it's a match made in picture-perfect heaven.

I know what people probably think when they see Luna and me walking down the hall together. Her tan skin, passed down from generations of people who first walked on this land. Her long, straight, midnight-black mane. Her perfectly round lips, and her tiny waist that rounds out at hips that Daniel loves to put his hands on. I'm sure other boys in school would love to put their hands on them, too.

Then, me.

Skinny, no curves.

Auburn hair that highlights with red and orange in the summer. Brown eyes. A few freckles that make themselves known when the sun hits me. Skin as pale as the Meade Lake snow.

I'm nothing more than "the friend."

But I'm okay with that. Because Luna Peake is a damn good friend. And the best part is, she doesn't care, either. She doesn't care what "status" her looks give her. She's the truest person I've ever known, and I know that no matter where she goes, she'll make sure I'm right there with her. Which brings me to our current situation.

"What about the swim meet?"

"Ugh. What about it?" I ask with a groan.

"It's the semi-finals. Our team is doing pretty well. Let's go and watch on Saturday morning!" she says. She's so excited that I can't help but smile, and she knows she's got me.

"Fine," I say.

LUNA PICKS me up way to fucking early for a Saturday, but luckily for her, she has a coffee in hand, ready and waiting for me when I get in. Kirby has to work early today, so it's just Luna and me. When we get to the aquatic center, the Meade Lake High section of the stands is already full, and I'm almost appalled at how many teenagers are willingly up this early to venture out into the Meade Lake cold to sit in a humid, chlorinated room for three hours.

"Baby!" Daniel hollers from up in the stands, and she waves excitedly as she leads me up the bleacher steps to him. He greets her with a tongue to the throat and then offers me a curt nod before we take our seats. Daniel is...odd. He doesn't really fit in with our group, and Lord knows we don't really fit into his. But Luna is Luna, and she can blur any line that comes in her way.

I watch a few of the events, and as the meet gets going, I actually find that I'm sort of invested. I stand with the crowd and join in some of the cheers. Who is this person I am becoming?

The swimmers are getting ready for the hundred-meter fly and that's when I hear a shrill voice shrieking from the top of the stands.

"Let's fucking *go*, Hunter!" It's Tommy Bills, the official clown of the sophomore class. Tommy is loud and rambunctious, but charming as hell, and fucking hilarious to top it off. Everyone in school knows Tommy. He leads the crowd in a "Let's go, Hunter!" cheer, and I follow their eyes down to the man himself—or boy, I should say. Shane Hunter. The sophomore phenom swimmer who's broken four school records already this season. I've seen him around. We had a class together freshman year.

But I've never really looked at him until today.

He's tall and skinny but with abs for days—that perfect swimmer's body. I can see every curve of every muscles as he stands in his navy-blue Speedo. He looks up at the crowd and gives us a quick smile and wink before rolling his swim cap on and stepping up to the line.

"Let's go, Hunter!" *Clap, clap, clap, clap, clap.*

Luna and Daniel have joined the ranks, but I'm still sitting, staring. Mesmerized by him. He fixes his goggles then leans forward to take position. When the alarm sounds, he dives in so gracefully that I forget to blink for a few seconds, and then, he's off like a damn torpedo. I watch him swim, lap after lap, flip after flip, until he's in the last stretch.

Every Meade Lake student, including me, is on their feet, screaming. I feel someone jump down and land next to me, and I realize it's Tommy.

"Let's. Fucking. Gooo!" he shouts, putting his arm around my neck and pulling me into him. I laugh and pull away from him, clapping my hands. Shane wins by a landslide, and I look carefully as he pulls himself out of the water.

"Party at Shane's tonight! Bring your friends!" Tommy starts shouting in all directions. He turns to me. "Grey, right?" he asks with a nudge of his shoulder. I nod. He's so busy being everyone's best friend that I had no idea he had the time to learn my name. "You know my boy, right?"

"Uh, I've heard the name. And now, I guess, I've seen him swim. Don't know that we've ever actually—"

"Shaneeeee! I fucking love you, man!" Tommy screams out, making me jump. Shane looks up at him and drops his head back, laughing hysterically as the parents and coaches stare up at us in disgust. Then Shane's eyes leap to me, and I feel my cheeks flush. I tuck a lock of my hair behind my ear.

"You're coming tonight, right?" Tommy asks.

"I, uh—"

"No, no. You're coming. You gotta meet my guy!" he says. And before I know it, he's got me by the hand, pulling me down the steps of the bleachers. He drags me across the pool deck where the rest of the team has cleared out. Shane reaches up and takes off his cap, shaking his shaggy hair back into place. Droplets of water slowly make their way down his bare back, and I clear my throat.

"My *man!*" Tommy shouts, holding his hand up and pulling Shane in for a bro hug. Shane laughs.

"Man, there's no missing you at these things," he says, shaking his head. Tommy laughs and stands back.

"Course not. You know I'm your biggest fan, shnookums," he says, lunging forward and playfully pinching Shane's cheeks. Shane laughs and shrugs him off. Then, his gray-blue eyes find mine. He clears his throat and stands a little taller. "Ah, my man, meet Grey."

"Grey?" Shane asks, an eyebrow lifted, and a half-smile on his round lips.

"Jules. Jules Grey," I say, tucking another piece of hair behind my ear.

"Hi, Jules Grey. We had a class together, right?" he asks. I nod.

"Yeah. I think so."

"Jules is coming tonight," Tommy tells him. "You're coming tonight, right?" He turns to me.

"I, uh——"

"Dude, tell her she's gotta come!" Tommy says before I can answer then springs in the direction of a pod of female swimmers. Shane is towel-drying himself before pulling some clothes out of his bag.

"So, you're coming tonight?" he asks. I shrug.

"I mean, I guess so?" I say. He laughs.

"Yeah, Tommy sort of makes the decisions for us. So, looks like I'll see ya tonight, Grey?" He gives me that half-smile again, and I feel my stomach flip.

"Looks like it."

"I can't believe that after *months* of practically begging you to do something, Shane and Tommy ask you to one party, and you say yes," Luna says as she leans over her bathroom sink, flicking on some mascara—not that she needs it.

"Tommy didn't really give me a chance to say no," I say with a chuckle.

"Ah, so that's the key, then?" she asks. I roll my eyes. A few seconds later, we hear a honk outside, and we grab our jackets and head for the door.

The perks of having a cousin that's a year older than you is that you almost always have a ride.

"Hey," Kirby says as she lays the passenger seat

down so that Luna can climb in the back. "So where is this shindig?"

"Shane Hunter's house," Luna says, tapping away on her phone.

"Daniel coming?" Kirby asks.

"Mhmm," she says. "I'm sure Derrick and Ryder will be there, too. Pretty much everyone."

I let out a breath of relief. At least my people will be there.

The Hunters live on Rich Man's Cove—it's actually called Pinebluff Cove, but one glance at a few of the houses, and it's clear that Rich Man's Cove makes more sense. Mr. Hunter is a doctor at a big medical center a few towns over and is sort of a Meade Lake success story. When we pull into the circle in front of the house, it's packed with cars.

Around the back of the house, we walk right into madness. A big group at a bonfire, another group playing cornhole.

"Hey, ladies!" we hear Tommy call as he walks toward us, double-fisting two beers as he makes his way to us. Tommy is shorter than Shane but still towers over me. He's got dark-brown hair and dark-brown eyes, but they always seem to be alight with his over-the-top zest for life.

"Hey, Tommy," Luna giggles. He takes her in for a long hug, and I watch her body grow stiff. Daniel walks up from the shore, and the air grows cold.

"Oh, sorry, my man," Tommy says, laying a gentle hand on Daniel's chest. Daniel all but growls before

Tommy takes his hand off. Dying to take the spotlight off Luna, I jump into Tommy's view.

"Miss me?" I ask.

"Ahh, my lady!" Tommy says, a look of relief on his face when he realizes he can spread the love elsewhere—this time, with no looming boyfriend to answer to. He gives Kirby a quick hug then leads us to the patio bar.

"Jules, hey," I hear Shane say from behind me, and my spine straightens. I whip around.

"Hey, Shane," I say.

"You made it," he says. "What can I get you guys?"

"Beer, stat," Kirby says. Shane smiles in her direction then reaches over the bar into the cooler on the counter and digs around till he finds one.

"And for you?" he says. I hold my hands up.

"I'm good for now, thanks," I tell him. After these last six months, cleaning up after my mom, drinking has sort of lost its luster. It also scares the shit out of me. He nods slowly then reaches over the counter for a red cup. He digs around in the cooler a little more and pulls out a Sprite. He pours it into the cup then hands it to me. I lift an eyebrow.

"Here, just carry this around," he says. "If anyone asks, it's got vodka in it. That way, you don't have to deal with these assholes bugging you to drink all night. Works every time," he says, holding his own red cup up. "Trust me."

I smile and take the cup from his hand.

"Genius."

Just then, we hear the roar of Tommy greeting someone else, and I realize it's Derrick

and Ryder. After they make their way through the rest of the crowd, they find me and Kirby at the bar.

"Hey, guys," Derrick says, putting a hand on my shoulder. I see Shane's eyes dart to it then back up quickly. "Hey, man, great job today."

Shane smiles and fist-bumps him.

"See you found our mother," Ryder says, grabbing a cup. Shane lifts an eyebrow.

"Jules, here," Derrick explains. "She's always keeping us in line."

"Someone has to watch out for you assholes," I tell them, and Derrick pulls me down into a headlock. We laugh as I struggle to get away from him, stumbling a bit. I fall forward just as Shane reaches out to catch me.

"Oh, yeah, and she's clumsy as shit, too," Kirby says, throwing back the beer she already finished. I roll my eyes, but when I look up, Shane's smiling.

"Great. So we gotta watch out for you, huh?" he asks.

"Pssh," Ryder says as he and Ryder turn toward the fire. "Lost cause!" I pretend to kick him, and he holds his hands up. "Kidding. Love you, Jules!"

I turn back to Shane.

"Good guys, those two," Shane laughs. I look in their direction.

"Pains in the ass," I laugh. "But fairly decent."

"You guys are good friends, then?" he asks. I shrug, leaning up against the bar.

"I mean, that whole group of us, we've been tight since elementary school. But I dunno; I don't always feel like I'm part of the group, even though I'm part of the group. Does that make any sense?" I ask, suddenly feeling a little self-conscious.

"Yeah, it makes sense," he says. He looks up at the

cornhole game that's going on, then over to the fire. "Whaddya say we start our own group?"

I look up at him and cock my head.

"What?"

"Misfits. We can go chill on the dock and pretend to drink," he says with a smile. I chuckle as we cheers our drinks.

"Misfits. Just, uh…just us?" I ask.

"For now," he says. "But Tommy will be with us soon." I shoot him a look.

"Tommy? No way. He's the life of the party," I say, looking over at Tommy sloppily hanging on a group of girls on the patio. Shane laughs.

"He is," he says. "But the life of the party isn't ever *really* part of the group, either."

I follow Shane down to the water, and we get to the edge of the dock and sit down. We talk for an hour or so about our families, school, swimming, my job at the cafe. And everything flows so easily that I forget there are thirty or so people just a few yards away. The crowd dissipates some, and then I hear feet across the wood of the dock.

"What are you two doin' down here all by your lonesome?" Tommy asks, sloppily making his way to us in a zig-zag line.

"Waitin' for you, jackass," Shane says. Tommy ruffles Shane's hair then plops down next to us. Tommy looks up at me, his eyes glazed over from hours of alcohol and being an entertainer.

"So, what's your story?" he asks, looking up at me as he dips his feet into the water. I shrug.

"No story, really," I lie. "Just your average Meade Lake lifer."

He raises an eyebrow at me, and I feel Shane's eyes on me, too.

"Lifer?"

"Yeah," I chuckle. "I'll probably die here at this water an old lady."

"You don't want to go anywhere? Explore the world a bit?" Shane asks. I look up at him.

"Of course I *want* to," I say with a shrug. "But wanting something and actually having it are two very different things."

"That's where you're wrong, my lady," Tommy says, throwing an arm around my shoulder. "You want it, take it."

4

I blink wildly for a minute, not sure it's really him I'm seeing.

His sandy hair is still disheveled, but in that sophisticated, purposeful way. His eyes are as deep and dark as I remember, and his square jaw is dusted with some stubble that reminds me how much time has passed since we've last seen each other. My jaw drops, and as it does, a smile tugs at the corner of his lips.

"Lookin' good, Grey," he says. It takes me a second to get myself together, the rush of everything I've felt toward him—the pain, the pleasure, the smiles, the absolute abandonment—pummeling like a freight train.

"Shane," I say when I finally collect myself. He takes his hands out of his pockets and slowly takes a step toward me, then another. Before I know it, I'm reaching to him and leaping into his arms. I wrap them around his neck as he lifts me off the ground. He squeezes me tight, and I can't believe how good it feels. When he sets me down again, I look up into his eyes.

They seem glazed over with something—some sort

of distant sadness, I think. I recognize it because I know mine show the same—because he left. But now, he's back.

"How…how have you—"

"So, Ty's getting married, huh?" I ask, cutting him off. I don't want him to ask me that question because I'm afraid that, even after all this time, I still won't be able to lie to him.

He swallows and narrows his eyes at me, taking the hint.

"Yeah, crazy. Jules, I—"

"So, uh, how long are you in town for?" I ask, cutting him off again. Nothing deep. Not here, not now. I'm not ready. I'm not sure if I ever will be.

"Not sure yet. I'm fully remote, so I can work from anywhere. Was planning to stay at least a few weeks to catch up with my folks some." I nod slowly.

"Wow, yeah, that's great."

Just as the awkward silence is lowering on us, I see Ty jogging across the parking lot toward us, all dressed in his suit and wedding ready.

"Hey, Jules!" he says, stopping to kiss my cheek. "How we looking?"

"Oh, it's all set up," I tell him. "The room looks great."

He smiles.

"Love to hear it. That's why I'm here. Instructed by the bride to do a last-minute check," he says with a wink. I smile. "Glad you two finally saw each other! Shane's been waiting to see you since I told him you were making the cake."

My eyes meet Shane's, and as they do, his drop to the ground.

"Listen, Jules, if you're not busy tonight, you should come," Ty says, his timing impeccable for disrupting the quiet again. My eyes jump to his.

"Oh, that's so sweet, but I wouldn't want to—"

"No, please. It would be so good for everyone to see you. Mom would *freak,*" he says, his hands on my shoulders. I look up to Shane again, and his eyes are big and pleading. I swallow and shake my head.

"That's so sweet of you," I say, "but I actually have another event tomorrow that I need to work on the cake for. I'll be back later, though, to pick up the platters. Thank you so much, Ty. That was really so sweet of you."

Ty nods and gives me one more squeeze. Shane takes in a deep breath, stuffing his hands back into his pockets. He's deadly in a suit, his body still slender and still with that same swimmer's definition. He cocks his head and gives me a nod, like he knows this moment is over.

"Have fun tonight, Shane," I tell him as I walk past.

"Jules," he says. I pause and look back. "It was really good to see you."

"You, too," I say before I practically run to the van.

I get in and slam the door shut, my hands shaking as I text Luna and Kirby.

I just saw him.

Who? Kirby asks.

Shane.

HOLY SHIT Luna responds. *How was it?!*

Weird as hell. Hopefully I won't see him again.

He better hope I don't see him EVER Kirby says.

I drop my head back to the seat and drive back to the shop.

THE HOURS SEEM to tick by as slow as ever, and I find myself checking the clock every five minutes. I finish a small sheet cake for another birthday party we have tomorrow and clean up the shop. Finally, it's eleven, and I know the wedding should be over by now. I get back in the van and head back to the resort. I go back in through the side door, and to my pleasant surprise, the room is almost cleared out, with only the remnants of a wild party left over. The deejay is still playing a few closeout songs, and at the corner of the room, I see Ty and his new wife talking to the catering manager. I sneak around to the back corner and slide what's left of the cake up off the silver platters, wiping them down and tucking them up under my arm.

"Oh, Jules!" Ty says. Damn it, spotted. "Baby, this is Jules, the cake maker."

The cake maker.

"Oh. My. GOD!" she says, running to me with open arms and wrapping them around me. She's tiny, like a perfect little cover model, with cascading blonde curls. Her makeup is impeccable with the exception of slightly smeared mascara. I can smell the wine on her breath as she hugs me.

"Jules, this is Blake, my wife," Ty says, his eyes beaming as he looks down at her. Yup, they're fucking perfect for each other.

"Hi, and congratulations!" I say. "You look abso-lutely beautiful."

"Oh, gosh," she says, sticking her bottom lip out and

putting a hand to her chest. "You're just the sweetest. And the cake was a hit! People loved it. We're giving your cards to *all* of our friends. Do you cater out near D.C.? It seems far, but it's not that far. Well, it's a little far, but not *too* far," she says, giggling over her drunken words. He smiles down at her and pulls her into him.

"She had a little too much fun tonight," he says. I nod and smile.

"The real fun will be happening momentarily in the newlywed suite," she says, grabbing his face in her hands and pulling him down for an extremely sloppy kiss. I clear my throat and look away.

"Well, on that note, I'll let you two go. Thank you so much for thinking of us," I say, "and congratulations again!"

They say their goodbyes, and I am more than relieved to get out of the room. I take in a deep breath and blow it out, happy for tonight to be over with.

"You came back," I hear Shane say, and I stop dead in my tracks. I turn back around and see him leaning up against the building, one foot up against the wall. He's holding his suit jacket off one finger behind his back, his tie is off, and his shirt is slightly unbuttoned. And *damn*, he doesn't look half bad.

"Yeah, to get the platters," I say, holding them up. "How was it?"

"It was exactly what Blake wanted," he says with a laugh. I smile and nod.

"Good, that's how it should be," I say. "Well, I'm gonna head back. It was good to see you, Shane."

I take a few steps toward the van again, trying to settle myself. In the background, I hear a slow song playing from the lodge.

"Jules," he says, and I turn back. He nods his head toward the music. "Dance with me?"

I freeze, my heart thumping so loud I'm sure he can hear it. His eyes are glazed over with a buzz, but right now, he looks strikingly sober. I look beyond him toward the lodge, the song blaring through the open door sending me way back, all those years ago. I close my eyes, letting the moment wash over me. Slowly, I open them, landing them right on his.

"Not tonight," I say, then I turn and get back in my van as fast as my legs will carry me.

5

THEN, WINTER OF SOPHOMORE YEAR

"Let's goooo!" I shout from the top of the stands as I bang my noise sticks together. Tommy's next to me, ringing his infamous cowbell and waving his hands in the air. It's the state semi-final meet, and so far, Shane has won every event he's swam in by a longshot. He's on the edge of the pool now, getting ready for his last event, the last leg of the four-hundred meter relay. A hush falls over everyone in the seconds before the buzzer goes off, and the first three legs are done in a flash. Meade High is in second place, and Shane takes his position. I always love to watch Shane's face just before he dives in. Stoic, like he hears nothing but the ripples in the water and sees nothing but the blue before him. Determined, an arrow to a target.

The buzzer blares, and we gawk at his usual perfection. Lap after lap, flip-turn after flip-turn. But Oakton High has their own secret weapon: Cooper Bowers. Shane has broken three of his statewide records so far, and word on the street is, Cooper's out for vengeance.

We all watch wide-eyed as they carve their way through the water. They're more than two laps ahead of everyone else, as if it's just the two of them in their own race. My heart jumps up to my throat as I watch Cooper match him with every wave of his arm and every kick of his feet.

"Come on, Shane! You got it, baby!" Tommy yells through cupped hands. I watch the lap counter on the wall.

Three laps.

Two laps.

One.

They're neck and neck.

And then Cooper wins.

Oakton's student section goes buck wild while ours sinks down into our seats.

"Damn," Tommy whispers. "He was so close."

Cooper offers Shane a handshake, then they pull themselves out of the pool. For the team, it doesn't matter much. They still made the state meet, and Shane qualified in all of his events. But as I watch him snatch his cap and goggles off and make his way to the locker room, I know my friend. I know that loss will haunt him until the state meet. I know that from the second Cooper's hand hit the wall, Shane became starved for victory.

It's one of the things I've grown to like about him over the last few months that we've been hanging out. He's a hell of a lot of fun, but he's also one of the most intense people I've ever met. It's a weird yet satisfying juxtaposition.

Tommy throws an arm over my shoulder.

"Let's go meet our guy," he says. I say goodbye to

Luna, Daniel, Derrick, and Ryder and follow Tommy down the bleachers and out the front door. We perch up against Tommy's truck where we always meet Shane—except, it's usually after a victory.

"We gotta have a party tonight," Tommy says. I shoot him a look. "No, I mean it. Still lots to celebrate. And we can't let him get too down."

I smile and nod.

One of the best parts about hanging with Tommy and Shane is their friendship. They've been best friends since they were six years old, when Shane's dad hired Tommy's to do their landscaping. Mrs. Hunter would always offer for Tommy to come with Mr. Bills so the boys could play. Tommy's mom died in a car accident when he was four, so Mr. Bills was raising him on his own. These two are the true definition of ride-or-die. And I'm pretty pleased to be a part of this group.

Finally, as most of the parking lot clears out, Shane makes his way from the side entrance of the building, his gray hoodie pulled up over his head. He has it unzipped, and I can see his bare chest peeking through.

"What, no shirt?" Tommy says with a laugh. Shane ignores him and throws his bag in the cab of the truck. "Hey, I'm talking to you."

Shane looks up at him as Tommy puts his hands on his shoulders.

"You've got fifteen minutes to mope, and then it's party time," he says. Shane rolls his eyes then looks at me.

"You killed it," I tell him. "And you'll get Cooper at States. I already can't wait."

A flicker of a smile crosses his lips as he opens the

truck door. I slide into my usual spot, right in the middle of both of them, and we head back to Shane's.

The Hunters take weekend trips when Dr. Hunter isn't working at the hospital, so it's not hard for us to get the house to ourselves. Tommy doesn't want to be home with his dad any more than I want to be home with my mom, so we find ourselves here most weekends, eating the food we never get at our houses, watching the premium channels we've only ever dreamed of.

We lie around all day while Shane stuffs himself full of enough calories to keep an elephant full for a week, replenishing what he burned off in the pool.

Finally, it's dark, and we know it's time.

Cars start pulling up, our friends rolling out of them like marbles on a hill.

"Let's do this, people!" Tommy says, grabbing a beer from the counter and tugging on his sweatshirt as he walks out the back door. I look at Shane.

"You don't really want a party tonight, do you?" I ask him. He smiles and shrugs.

"I'm not really in the mood," he says.

"Say our hellos then hide at the dock?" I ask with a smirk. He bites his bottom lip and nods.

"Deal."

He follows me out the back door and underneath the deck where everyone has made themselves comfortable on the patio. There are more people than I was expecting for it being so cold out, but it's Meade Lake, and people aren't afraid of a little chill.

"There he is!" Ryder says, smacking him on the back.

"Dude, you were so close in that last race," Derrick says, settling into an Adirondack chair. Shane nods.

"That kid was so fucking fast!" someone else hollers.

"Oh my God, that Cooper kid? Fast as shit," someone else says. I cross my arms over my chest and eye them all down.

"Hope he enjoyed his last win," I say then look at Shane. He gives me that half-smile and nods lightly in my direction. When the conversation takes another turn, I see him grab for two red cups, filling them with Sprite. But as he's walking in my direction, I see Ricky Dawes out of the corner of my eye, and he's making his way toward me.

Ricky is just...slimy. His dad owns a few of the marinas in town, making them some of the other occupants of Rich Man's Cove. His dad walks behind counters of businesses he doesn't own, and his catchphrase should be *They know me here*. All qualities he's passed down to his son.

The obnoxious thing about Ricky is that, barring his personality, he's a good-looking dude. Tricky to the unsuspecting female. But once he opens his mouth, it pretty much gives him away.

He hit on Luna last week, something that caught him a snatched collar by Daniel, and the week before that, it was Tanya Smart. He's like some sort of horny magnet that we all wish would just go away.

"What we havin' tonight, Grey?" he asks, slipping an arm around my neck and peering down into my cup.

"It's, uh—"

But before I pass off with our usual fib, he snatches it out of my hand and takes a swig.

He slams it down on the bar next to me and wipes his lip.

"It's just fucking soda," he says, loud enough that the people around us all turn in our direction. "Nah, no way. Get this girl something *real.*"

I feel the eyes on me, and while I'm not afraid to stand up to your average peer pressure, I just don't *want* to. I don't want the judgment; I don't want to have to explain myself. And I know I shouldn't have to.

Even Tommy and Shane don't know the full story. They know it has to do with my parents, but I haven't even brought them to my house yet, let alone let them meet the trainwreck that is my mother.

No one should have to experience that.

"I'm good," I mutter quietly.

"No way, no *way,*" he says, pulling me into him closer. "This lady here needs a drink!"

I roll my eyes as I strain to pull away from him.

"I don't want anything," I say again, this time a little more sternly.

"She said she's good," I hear Shane's voice say, booming above the rest of the chatter. Ricky's eyes land on him, piercing through him as a sly smile spreads across his lips. And as he burns holes through Shane with his eyes, he pulls me back into him, even closer.

"Saving this one for yourself, are we, Hunter?" Shane swallows, his eyes narrowing, and everything gets quiet.

"Let go of me, Ricky," I say, not liking the dialogue that's going on around me, as if I'm not even here.

"Aw, come on, Jules. Stick with the real winner. Your bud here's only second-best, anyhow," he says.

"Ricky, let—"

Boom.

Shane shoves him so hard that we both stumble backward, Ricky to the ground, and me into a crowd of people at the bar. Derrick steadies me, then he and Ryder lunge forward to survey the damage.

Ricky's still lying on the ground, staring up at Shane.

"Can you not hear?" Shane says, his chest heaving as he leans down closer to Ricky. "I think she said she wanted you to let go."

Ricky stands slowly, taking a step back first then lunging back at Shane.

And then all hell breaks loose.

Fists and blood and curse words are flying. Derrick and Ryder jump in to try and split them up, and Tommy comes running up from the group of girls he was entertaining on the grass.

"Hey, hey, hey!" he shouts. He jumps in, pulling the two off of each other, helping Derrick hold Shane back. I cover my mouth as Luna wraps an arm around me. Shane has blood dripping from his eyebrow, but Ricky looks like he got hit by a truck.

"What the fuck is going on?" Tommy asks.

"Ask Dawes," Shane growls.

Ricky spits and wipes the blood from his lips.

"What the fuck's the matter with you, Hunter?" he asks. He turns slowly, as if to accept his defeat, but pauses. "She must have a golden pussy or something."

My eyes go from Ricky back to Shane, and I watch as something sets him off. He lunges across the patio again, but before he can reach Ricky, Tommy, Derrick, and Ryder pull him back.

"Shane, Shane," Tommy says, standing directly in front of him, taking his face in his hands. "Calm down, man. It's all good. Calm down."

I watch as Shane draws in a few sharp breaths, his eyes slowly losing their glaze of rage. Once Tommy's sure Shane's calm, he turns back to Ricky.

"I believe what my friend was trying to say was—"

Boom.

Tommy lands the hardest punch I've ever seen right on Ricky's jaw, sending him flying to his back on the patio. He leans down so he's just inches from Ricky's face as the crowd around us gasps and cheers.

"Get the fuck outta here, Dawes," he says. "And leave my friends alone."

Ricky's minions, who were shockingly helpless during the entire ordeal, pull him to his feet and lead him around to the front of the house. Tommy turns to everyone.

"Alright, peeps," he shouts, "let's get back to it!"

As everyone goes on about their night, I walk toward Shane. Tommy gets to both of us and throws his arms around our necks.

"Let's go down to the water," he says. "Jules, you take Mr. Hothead in and clean up that eyebrow, and then let's go down to the dock. I'm gonna go say hello to a few people, and I'll meet ya."

AFTER WE PUT peroxide on the cut on his eyebrow and stick a bandage on it, we head back outside to meet Tommy. The walk to the end of the dock is quiet while I'm searching for what to say. We sit down at the end of it, the cold air from the water sending a chill down my spine.

"Thank you for that," I say to him after a few more

minutes. He nods, staring out at the black water. "Are you...are you okay?"

In the few months that we've been friends, I've never seen Shane like this. He nods.

"I'm sorry, Jules," he says. I cock my head. "I shouldn't have let him get to me like that. But you told him no, and I just didn't like that he had his hands on you…"

His voice trails off, and I see his knuckles turn white as he clenches his fist. I reach out and give his hand a quick squeeze.

"Don't apologize," I tell him. "You got him off of me, didn't you?"

He nods.

"Yeah. But I try real hard not to ever get…"

"Get like what?"

"Like my father."

I turn my head to him and lift an eyebrow.

"Your dad? Sweet, calm Dr. Hunter?" I ask. He smiles as he looks at me.

"No. My father. Roger Doyle. Angry, belligerent, drunkard Mr. Doyle who couldn't keep his hands off my mom."

My eyes grow wide.

"We left when I was four and Ty was six," he says. "And my mom moved us here. She met dad—Dr. Hunter—shortly after, and the rest is history. When they got married, he legally adopted Ty and me."

I nod.

"Wow," I say.

"Luckily, Dad came into our lives right when we needed him. He did all the heavy lifting when it came to raising us. But there are some things I still remember about Roger. Things he did to my mom. Even when she told him not to."

His voice gets quiet, and I see him swallow. I scoot closer to him and tuck my arm through his.

"You don't look like a Doyle," I tell him. "You look like a Hunter, to me."

_____

6

"The fuck you mean he asked you to *dance*?" Kirby says, so exasperated that the fry she's eating falls out of her mouth. I'm lying on my couch with my arm draped over my eyes while she scarfs down her late-night, post-shift snack.

"Yep. Right there in the parking lot," I say, pushing myself up and reaching to sneak a fry from her plate.

"I mean, if it wasn't *him*, that's actually romantic as fuck," Kirby says, and I laugh.

"I can't believe he's back," I mutter quietly as I sink back down into the cushion.

"I know. How ya feelin' about it?" she asks. I lie back and stare up at the ceiling, letting out a long breath through pursed lips.

"I feel…" My voice trails off. I don't really know. I felt *so* many things when I first saw him. Like how fucking good it felt to wrap my arms around him for a minute. And how fucking mad I was at him for abandoning me. And how much gratitude I still have for him in my heart for what he did for me that night.

Like I said, *so* many things. Too many to put into words.

"Yeah, that's sorta what I figured," Kirby says, and I look at her. "That guy was your whole world. Him and Tommy. And then, in an instant, your world changed. But now he's back. I'm sure you're all over the place."

I nod.

Thanks, Kirb, for saying what I couldn't.

"Don't worry. I'm sure he'll be gone soon, and you can get back to your life," she says, clapping the salt off her hands and standing up. "I'm gonna go get some sleep. See ya at Derrick's tomorrow."

"Night, Kirb," I say, following her to the door and locking it behind her. I lean back against the wood of the door.

He'll be gone soon, and you can get back to your life.

Yeah, that's exactly what I need to do. I've come too far to make a U-turn now.

I SPEND the next day lying around the house, blasting music while I pick up a bit, and thoroughly enjoying my time in my underwear on my day off. Living by myself has some major perks, and this is definitely one of them. But it's finally time to get ready to go to Derrick's for a fire, so I reluctantly make my way to my room to pull on my comfiest yoga pants and my favorite hoodie, and I throw my rust-colored locks into some sort of octopus-looking creature on the top of my head.

It's finally cold enough for boots, so I slip on my favorite pair and head out the door.

Derrick lives with his wife, Kaylee, in this giant house that Kaylee inherited from her grandmother.

Kaylee joined the crew a little over a year ago, but it feels like she's been here a lot longer. Same with Ryder's wife, Mila. Mila was around when we were kids when her family came up for summers, and she made her way back to Meade Lake later.

A lot of people seem to do that.

They go, but they come back.

As I pull in, Mila is parking their car in the driveway and hopping out. I beat her to the passenger door where I open it and squeeze Ryder's shoulders. He turns to me and pops his cane out, feeling his way to the ground.

"Lookin' handsome as always," I say, nudging him as he gets out. He flashes me a silly smile.

"Do I? I haven't seen myself in a few years," he says. Mila and I laugh as I close the door behind him and follow them around the side of the house. Ryder lost his vision a few years back, and it was tough for a while. But we've all tried our best to help him adjust. When it first happened, Mila told him he was more than just his eyes. And a few years later, we all know she was absolutely right.

I smile as we make our way around to the back patio where Derrick already has the fire started. Luna sits with her knees tucked up under her, Derrick pokes at the fire, and Kaylee is serving hot chocolate. Mila and Ryder pull their chairs up, and Kirby is refilling her wine glass. These are my people.

"There she is," Luna says, nodding her head in my direction. "Heard you had a little parking lot run-in."

My eyes dart to Kirby, who innocently shrugs her shoulders.

"A run-in? With who?" Mila asks, snuggling up next to Ryder.

"Shane's back," Luna says. Everyone gets quiet for a moment, and I feel all eyes on me. I clear my throat and grab a stick to poke at the fire.

"You saw him?" Mila asks. I nod.

"Yeah. At the hotel. We made Ty's cake. It was really awkward," I say, stuffing my hand in my pocket. "Glad it's over."

"Yikes. Maybe I should sneak back out then," Shane says, and everyone turns to whip their heads in his direction. I feel my heart rate instantly pick up, my eyes like saucers.

"Sorry, Jules. I, uh, ran into Shane in town and invited him tonight. Didn't have a chance to mention that," Derrick says sheepishly next to me. I shoot him a look as everyone jumps up from their chairs and greets him. Everyone except Kirby.

My dear, sweet, loyal-as-hell cousin.

I sit awkwardly as they exchange hugs and kisses, telling him how good he looks, asking how he's been. Derrick pulls up a chair next to him—to his credit, it's on the complete opposite side of the fire from me—and introduces him to Kaylee.

I watch as he asks every single person around the fire how they've been. When he gets to Ryder, he looks down at the ground.

"I'm so sorry I haven't been back sooner to check in on ya, man," he says.

"Hey, man, no problem. We all have lives! Besides, the grocery delivery you sent was a godsend!"

I look up at Shane then back to Ryder. *Grocery delivery?*

Finally, Shane's eyes land on Kirby.

My cousin is the polar opposite of me with dark-brown, corkscrew curls, round hips, and the biggest boobs this side of the Appalachian Mountains. She's sitting with her legs crossed, lips pursed, and daggers coming out of her eyes, pointed right in his direction.

"How you been, Kirb?" he asks. She looks him up and down and sucks her teeth, and I can practically hear everyone around us draw in a breath, waiting for her response.

"How have I been?" she asks, leaning forward. "You're gonna just take off for, like, a fucking decade, and we're just supposed to be excited to see you?"

Everyone's eyes are as round as the moon, and I can feel my heartbeat reverberating in my throat.

Finally, she leans back, a smile tugging at her lips. Everyone lets out a breath of relief. But then she leans forward again.

"But seriously," she says before sitting back again. Shane swallows nervously, leaning back in his chair. For the next few hours, I stay as quiet and invisible as possible. Partially because I'm still getting used to him being here, but also because I don't want to share too much. He's gone more than ten years without knowing anything about me. Why should he get to know anything now?

Kaylee brings down fixings for s'mores and starts divvying them out. Everyone lunges for sticks and marshmallows but me. I sit back and look around. Kaylee is perched on Derrick's knee as he nuzzles the back of her neck. Mila and Ryder keep sneaking kisses, and Luna and Kirby haven't stopped talking about how much things have changed since Shane left. Every few minutes, I feel his eyes on me, but I haven't looked at him. Not once.

I see him stand out of the corner of my eye, but I turn to Luna to ask her something unimportant about her mom's shop.

From around me, I see a stick with a marshmallow on the end appear, black and charred.

"Burnt to a crisp," Shane says, kneeling down next to me. "Just the way you like them."

I take it slowly and look at him.

"I can't believe you remember that."

"I didn't forget anything about you, Jules."

7

THEN, WINTER OF SOPHOMORE YEAR

"Hold still," Luna says to me as I shiver in the parking lot, holding up my shirt as she meticulously paints "SH" on my stomach in dark-blue paint.

"Hurry up," I say behind quivering lips, "it's f-fucking f-freezing out here."

Luna finishes with one last swipe of her finger then stands back and gives me a look.

"Don't be such a baby," she says. "Alright, Tommy, you're up!"

We're all here, ready to cheer Shane on today, and although we're all laughing and joking around, I woke up with this knot in my belly for him. I know how badly he wants this, to beat Cooper. I think I might want it even more.

After Luna finishes painting cheeks and stomachs and backs, we all grab our posters and head inside. It's much more packed than normal, with bandwagon fans jumping in cars to cheer on Shane and the rest of the team. Everyone's settling into the student section of the bleachers, and Tommy is already leading chants and cheers before the team is even out to do their warmup laps. But I am just staring ahead at the empty pool, waiting. This race could be big for Shane. This could put him on the map for next season when college recruiters can actually start pursuing him.

College.

Leaving Meade Lake.

It seems so far away right now.

And as I feast my eyes on the boy who has quickly become the biggest part of my life, I'm okay with keeping it that way.

Far off in the comfortable distance.

We watch and cheer as the teams warm up and grow quiet when Shane and Cooper exchange icy glances.

As the meet goes on, Meade High wins every single relay, and Shane has won each of his individual races.

Up till this one. His last race. The one that Cooper is in. Shane's standing at the block, jumping up and down on his toes, cocking his head from side to side. He stretches his arms overhead, then down to his feet, out to his sides, shaking them to get limber. Then, slowly, he lifts his eyes up to the stands. To me.

I swallow and stand so he can see me better, and I nod. He nods back then blows out a long breath just as the first buzzer goes off. They line up on their blocks, and I watch as every muscle in his back clenches. Then it goes off, and he dives into the water like a swan.

I feel a hand slide down and snake around mine.

"He's got this," Tommy whispers. I squeeze his hand back and nod as we both start screaming Shane's name.

It's close. Too close for comfort.

Shane and Cooper are neck and neck, their arms moving in sync with every single lap.

But then, Shane's an inch farther ahead. And then another inch. And then something happens, and he kicks it into another gear. And suddenly, Cooper can't keep up.

"Let's go, Shane!" I call out.

"Yes, Shane!" Tommy says. "Get after it, Shane!"

"Wooo! Go, Shane!" I hear Tanya say from a few rows back. "My God, he's hot as hell."

I whip my head around and look at her, but she's staring down, biting her lip with fake anticipation.

I don't know why, but it bothers me. I shake it off and turn back to the pool just as Shane is turning into his last lap. He's like a torpedo in the water, moving faster and faster.

And then Shane reaches his arm out and touches the wall. We wait one second, two seconds, three seconds, and then Cooper hits it.

Our boy won by a landslide.

Tommy's screaming, turning around to pick me up and swirl me around.

"Let's. Fucking. Go!"

There's a mad rush to the bottom of the bleachers as Shane pulls himself out of the pool. The rest of the swim team jumps him, throwing him up on their shoulders. I clap and cheer and smile like an idiot. My best friend is a state champ.

We wait in the parking lot for him to come out, which he does, per usual, after everyone else. Finally, we see him walk through the glass doors, his parents on one side of him and a man in a USC jacket on the other. They're smiling, and then they stop to make a little more small-talk and then go their separate ways. He kisses his mom and fist-bumps his dad before finally making his way to us. We all bumrush him, high-fiving and hugging and laughing, and then it's my turn. I jump into his arms, inhaling that familiar smell of his shampoo with the remnants of the chlorine that's left in his hair.

"You fucking did it!" I say.

"You told me I would," he mutters with a chuckle. "That was partially for you, Jules." I pull back from him slowly, trying to get a gauge on his expression. *What does this mean?* He slides me down his body slowly until my feet hit the ground. "You're my best friend."

He nudges me playfully then turns to Luna and Tommy, pulling them both in for hugs.

It means you're just his best friend, dumbass.

"Did you see the look on Cooper's face? Classic, man. Classic," Tommy says. "Anyway, you know what this means! Your parents still goin' out of town tonight?"

Shane nods with a smile.

"Course. You wouldn't catch them dead in Meade Lake on a weekend."

"You heard the man. Party tonight at Hunter's!" Tommy shouts as he walks toward the truck. Shane throws an arm around my neck as we follow behind.

"You're comin' tonight, right?" he asks.

"Hmm, I'm not sure. I might have to rearrange my sock drawer tonight," I tell him with a sly smile. He scrunches up his nose and shakes his head before he opens the passenger door and lets me slide in first.

We get brunch at Perry's Pancake House, shouting and embarrassing Shane in the parking lot as we celebrate his victory. He laughs and shakes his head, those deep-blue eyes beaming with pride and adoration for us.

The way I feel when I'm with him and Tommy, I've never felt before. Just truly and purely happy.

After we eat, we go back to Shane's and set up a bit. We bring up firewood from the giant shed at the back corner of the yard, set the chairs up around the fire pit, and carry out bottles of liquor from Mr. Hunter's bar. It's fucking freezing outside, but Meade Lakers are no sissies. We'll sit out here all night, drink and eat our weight in marshmallows and chips, and then we'll all crash inside like we do just about every weekend.

We run out to the store to finish up the last of the junk-food buying. Tommy makes a beeline for the soda aisle to get whatever mixers he needs, and Shane and I head for the chips. As we're walking, he nudges me with the cart. I shove him back, and he nudges me again. He looks down at me and gives me that half-smile, and I turn and shake my head, beaming like a fucking goon. I don't know why Shane Hunter makes me like this, but I don't want it to stop.

"I'm still reeling from today," I tell him as we round the corner. "You were so—"

"Well, if it isn't the champ himself!" Tanya says, just as she's grabbing a bag of chips off the top shelf, her shirt rising up above her midriff. I freeze where I stand, but Shane lets go of the cart—*our* cart—and walks over to help her grab it.

"Hey," he says as she bats her eyelashes and stands up on her tip-toes to give him an over-the-top hug.

"I know I already told you this outside the locker room, but you were *amazing* today," she says with a slow brush of his arm. "Seriously!"

"Thanks," he says, a little bashfulness taking over. "You comin' tonight?"

I feel a little fire in my belly.

"Wouldn't miss it," she says with a quick smile and a nibble of her bottom lip. She walks by, her hips swaying back and forth as she cuts between us. "Oh, hey, Jules."

"Hey, Tanya," I say.

"See you tonight," she hollers over her shoulder.

Shane watches her walk away and only stops when I clear my throat.

"What?" he asks. I snatch a bag of chips from the shelf and chuck them at him. He laughs as he catches it.

"Wipe your damn drool," I tell him as I walk by, pushing the cart.

I force a playful smile, but it's not all that funny to me.

This shit happens a lot. But I guess that's what happens when you're the best friend of the big man on campus. You're one of the guys. Not one of the girls he watches walk away in the grocery store. The last relationship Shane was in was with a girl at Oakton High, but they broke up shortly before he and I met. He hasn't dated anyone since, but that's not to say he doesn't enjoy his fair share of female attention.

"Aww, you know you're my girl, Jules," he says, grabbing me and pulling me into him and squeezing me into a dramatic hug. I laugh as I pretend to push him off, but honestly, being pressed up against his hard chest isn't the worst thing in the world.

"Yeah, yeah, whatever," I laugh, shaking him off and pushing the cart toward Tommy.

"You guys ready?" he asks. "I just saw Tanya. She's coming tonight. *Damn*, she's fine."

Shane raises his eyebrows at me and shrugs, and I roll my eyes as we go through the checkout line. Shane always pays, no matter where we are or what we're doing. I tried to argue him on it once, but he said his dad once told him, "Never let a friend buy what you can afford to pay for." I assumed it was his dad's money, but then I found out that Shane and Tommy took jobs at the arcade last year. Mr. Hunter might have the means to fund his sons' galivanting, but he doesn't. They work for their own galivanting.

We finish setting up, and I look around.

"This looks like the rager of all ragers. Fit for a swimming king," I tell Shane. He chuckles and shakes his head.

"I'm only a sophomore. I'm more like a duke right now," he says. Tommy comes out of the bedroom in a new polo and jeans, with a hoodie over his finger as if it's a fancy suit jacket. I laugh, but I wouldn't mind changing myself.

"Tom, can you run me home real quick?"

He shoots me a look as he checks the time.

"I just want to change real fast."

"I'll take you," Shane says, and Tommy and I both snap to look at him.

"It's *your* party," I say. Shane lifts an eyebrow at me.

"Maybe. But who are they really here to see? Besides, we'll be right back. Hold down the fort, Tom," Shane says, grabbing his keys off the counter. "Let's go, Grey."

"You got it," Tommy says, sinking into the Hunters' huge sectional and happily flipping through the channels as if he owns the place.

"I'll be fast," I tell Shane as I pull the seatbelt around me. He shrugs.

"I'm in no rush," he says.

We pull out of the Hunters' neighborhood and make the few right turns it takes to get to my house. A small little house that's only three miles from Shane's but might as well be on a different planet. The gutter hangs low on the right side, and the grass is a little taller than it should be. A broken-down pickup truck that's missing the back tire sits in the back of the driveway—one of the glorious things my dad left when he took off.

Mom's old Chevy sits crooked next to it, and I wonder how many drinks she had before she parked it there. Shane and Tommy rarely come to my house; I try to avoid it whenever possible. Just for quick trips like this, until I get my license. Then I'll take her car, and maybe *that* will stop her from driving while intoxicated since a few DUIs and a court order can't seem to.

"I'll be right back," I tell him as I unbuckle. I silently cross my fingers that Mom is asleep already, so I won't have to exchange any words.

But when I walk in, I wish I had never come back.

I smell something burning and look to see the stove on, whatever was cooking now black and charred. There are seven empty beer bottles on the counters, two more on the table, and one half-nursed one slipping from her hand. She's passed out on the couch with her mouth open, a slice of uneaten pizza clutched in her other hand.

And I know my plans have changed.

I sigh, biting my lip so I don't cry before I send Shane away. I walk back to the door and out to the car. He smiles, then a puzzled look crosses his face as he puts down his window.

"I, uh, I actually think I need to stay in tonight," I

tell him. One eyebrow goes up as he turns his music down.

"What? Why?"

"My mom, uh, isn't feeling too good…"

My voice trails off, and so do my eyes. I can't look at him and lie.

"Jules, what's goin' on?"

"Nothing," I tell him. "You should go back. I'll see you guys tomorrow," I say. I turn back to the house, but I hear his ignition turn off.

He gets out and shuts the door.

"Jules, tell me what's going on," he says, positioning himself in front of me. I take in a deep breath, but I can't say anything. I just shake my head and bite my lip, looking off into the woods. He walks around me, and I reach for him. But I miss. He marches up the front steps and into the house, me right on his tail. My heart is beating so fast I feel faint.

Shane has learned a lot about me over the last few months. But he hasn't seen *this*. He doesn't know exactly why I don't drink. He doesn't know what my life at home looks like.

Until now.

And I'm afraid once he sees *this*, he'll never see *me* the same way.

He freezes a few feet from the couch, looking down at my mom then looking around at all the empty bottles. I see his shoulders heave up and down, then he slowly reaches up and takes his coat off, slipping it over the back of one of the chairs.

"Do you have trash bags?" he asks as he pushes his sleeves up. My eyes widen.

"What?"

"Let's get this cleaned up," he tells me. I shake my head.

"No," I tell him. "You need to go. People are waiting for you."

"Yeah, well. None of those people are you, now, are they?"

Our eyes meet again, and I don't know a time when we've had this stone-cold seriousness between us.

"Shane…"

"I'm not leaving you here with this," he cuts me off.

"But I can't leave her at all tonight," I tell him. "I have to stay and make sure she doesn't choke."

His eyes are saucers now as he looks down at me. He wasn't ready to see this. He wasn't ready to see me like this.

"Choke?"

"Yes. If she gets sick, she could choke on it. It's happened before. I have to stay up and make sure she doesn't."

He grabs a few bottles off the counter and turns to me.

"Guess we'll need some energy drinks then, huh?"

He flashes me a smile, and for a brief moment, I feel like the world is crashing down around me like it has so many times since my dad took off. I never know who to blame when this happens. I could so easily blame my dad. He left. He took off, the only one bringing in any solid income, and has yet to offer a cent to us. He left without so much as a word to me and a *lot* of hateful words toward my mom. He couldn't take the wasted days, the binging nights, the bills not getting paid on time. So he left. I hate all those things too, but he never even gave me the option to leave with him.

But my mom has always been a drinker. That's part of the reason my dad left in the first place. And she's never made an effort to get better. In fact, all she's done is let herself get worse. I know addiction is a disease. I just wish I were enough to be her cure.

I throw the last of the bottles in the recycling bin and wipe down the counters and the table. I slip the slice of pizza out of Mom's hand and throw it away. Shane comes back in from taking the trash out and looks around.

"What else can I do?" he asks. I look around then down at my mom.

Ugh. I hate what I need him to do next.

"I need to get in her bed and roll her on her side," I say to him, wanting to curl up in a ball and die. He nods and, without hesitating, walks to my mom and scoops her up like it's no sweat. Actually, I think it *is* no sweat.

I lead him down the hall to her room and pull down the covers. He lays her gently on the mattress and helps me turn her to her side, then I pull the covers up around her. Once he's back in the hall, I bend to leave a quick kiss on her forehead like I have so many times before.

Maybe tomorrow will be better, Mama.

When I walk back out to the living room, he's on the couch, pointing the remote at the T.V. screen and scrolling through channels. I sort of like how he looks here. Like he's at home.

I plop down next to him and pull my feet up underneath me. He's learned so much about me tonight, and yet, he doesn't seem fazed.

"Shane, you really don't have to stay. I'm sorry I can't celebrate with you tonight. I feel so bad—"

"Jules, stop," he says, dropping the remote and

turning to me. "Where do we end up at every single party we have?"

I look up at him through shamed eyes.

"The dock."

He nods.

"This is the dock tonight," he says, motioning to the living room. "And I don't wanna be anywhere else. I'm celebrating my win with my best friend."

It's been so long since someone has put me first—including my own mother.

"She's, uh, she's had a really hard time ever since my dad left," I tell him. "I guess we both have, just in different ways. It's been almost a year now, and he hasn't reached out once. I never thought we meant so little to him."

He reaches out and takes my hand.

"Jules, anyone who doesn't fight to stay in your life doesn't deserve to have you in theirs," he says.

I look at him, narrowing my eyes, trying desperately to fight back the tears.

I bite my lip, but it's no use. They come hard and fast, with a vengeance. Months of pent-up tears that have been waiting to be dried by someone else.

"Jules, hey," he says, sliding across the couch toward me. He wraps his arms around me and pulls me into him so that my head is cradled against his chest. He leans back on the couch so that all my weight can rest on him. And I cry. I'm not sure how much time passes, but when I finally take in a long breath, his shirt is soaked beneath my face. When he feels me slowing down, he lifts me off of him, cupping my face in his hands.

He looks right into my eyes, his deep, gray-blue on

my brown, honing in on them. Like he's asking some-thing and telling me something at the same time.

"You deserve better than this, Jules," he whispers. I swallow. "You're meant for so much more than this."

I rest my head back against his chest and let my heavy eyes close. And for the first time in months, I believe that.

8

I close my eyes and lean my head back in the crisp, fall breeze, letting it blow through my copper-colored waves and send a chill down my spine. I used to crave that chill, that feeling of impending winter. It used to be my favorite season. Now, I can hardly look at snow without feeling sick.

It's the last boat ride of the season today, a tradition our crew started when we were teenagers. The very last ride before all the boats get lifted out of the water, before the docks are pulled up, before the freezing temperatures transform the lake into a winter wonder-land. At least, they used to. Now, it feels more like a wasteland.

I'm perched on the end of the community dock across from the shop that Derrick and Ryder own together, waiting for the rest of them to get here. I'm early to everything, but it pays off on mornings like this, with the sky streaked purple and pink, a light layer of fog slowly creeping back off the water and into the black mountains. I smile.

This is part of the reason why I never left this place.

"There she is," I hear Derrick say as he leads the crew down the wooden staircase to the docks. "Ready?" he asks.

"Always. Mornin', guys," I say, nodding to Kaylee, Luna, Ryder, and Mila. I bend down to give Annabelle's head a ruffle and then follow them to the boat and help Derrick untie it as Mila helps Ryder on board.

He feels his way with his cane then chucks it onto the boat as he climbs in.

It's almost second nature for Mila to act as his eyes now, but with every day that passes, Ryder gets a little more adamant about keeping his independence. It's tough to watch him struggle, but there's also so much beauty in watching him do little things on his own. Watching those little traces of his dignity being built back up again.

Everyone climbs on board and takes their seats, waiting to push off. But Derrick turns up toward the steps.

"There he is," he says. We all turn, and my stomach drops.

"Sorry I'm late," Shane says, doing a light jog across the dock while holding up a cupholder full of coffees. "Thought everyone could use a little pick-me-up."

"Oh, that's so nice of you!" Kaylee says, happily grabbing for one of the cups. Mila takes the rest and passes them around as he climbs on board, our eyes finding each other like magnets.

Derrick gives me a guilty look then turns to start his boat.

Shane takes the seat directly across from me.

"Morning, Jules," he says.

"Mornin'," I say.

"Coffee?" he asks. I shake my head.

"No, thanks." *You're not doing me any favors, Hunter.*

"I, uh, was telling Shane we were going on the last ride today. Thought it would be fun. Like old times." Derrick chuckles nervously then kicks up the speed and happily turns forward.

You'll pay for that, traitor.

After a few minutes of awkward silence, Ryder calls Shane up to the front of the boat. It immediately feels like a weight has been lifted, like I can take a breath. I lean back against the side of the boat and let my head drop back. My nose and cheeks are already frozen from the chilly lake air, but this is when I'm in my element. I feel a nudge against my leg, and I open my eyes.

"You okay?" Luna asks, scooting in next to me.

"Oh, yeah," I say. "Just trying to enjoy what's normally one of my favorite days of the year." My eyes flick up to Shane at the front of the boat. Even in a big hoodie, he's so toned it's obnoxious. His thick, sandy locks are blowing in the wind, and those blue-gray eyes are striking, even at this distance. He's laughing with Ryder about something, and for a second, everything but sheer joy that he's here seems to melt away.

But we hit a wake, jolting us a little bit, and I remember the hurt.

"I still just can't believe he's here," I mutter quietly, grabbing a blanket from my bag and pulling it around me. Luna lifts it and tucks herself under it next to me.

"I know," she says with a sigh. "I'm sorry. I know it's gotta be weird."

"It is."

"Well, if it's any consolation, I don't think he'll be

here long," Kaylee chimes in from the passenger seat. We whip our heads to her, unaware she was listening. She bites her lip sheepishly. "Sorry. Close quarters."

"What makes you say that?" I ask, trying to not sound so eager. Kaylee looks over to Derrick, who is very preoccupied with driving the boat and talking to the front crew. She gets up and joins us on the backseat.

"Well, he told Derrick that, while he's here, he's meeting with a few real estate guys in the area." Her eyes drop to her hands.

"Like, to buy some?" I ask. Kaylee shakes her head.

"No. On behalf of his company. That's what he does for a living."

"What real estate guys?" Luna asks behind clenched teeth. Oh, God. This could be bad. Kaylee clears her head and scoots closer to us.

"I don't know who all of them are, but I, uh, I know that one of them is Reed Miller."

I swallow and turn slightly to Luna. Her eyes narrow, and her jaw twitches.

Reed Miller is the son of Walt Miller, of Miller Mountain Real Estate. Walt grew up in Meade Lake like the rest of our parents did and realized that the untouched land in the area was a gold mine. He began buying up huge plots of it in his early twenties then selling it off piece by piece. And that was how his empire was born. He expanded it by adding a vacation rental company later on, and he still dabbles in commercial and residential real estate in the area. When he made his first fortune, he moved to a gigantic mansion on the southernmost end of the lake then shipped his kids, Reed and Riley, to a private school an hour away.

For almost thirty years, Walt Miller and his company

have been trying to swallow up whatever is left of Meade Lake's undeveloped and unclaimed land.

One of the most prized properties is the north side of Meade Mountain. The mountain that Luna's family lives on, where they have their business. The mountain where their people lived off the land, grew their crops, raised their children. The mountain that is the only thing that remains of her people.

It's safe to say that Luna *hates* the Miller family.

"What the *fuck?*" she mutters. Kaylee swallows and looks around. She's still the newest one to the crew, so she's still a little unsure of where she fits in.

"I'm, I'm not sure what the deal is, or if he's going through with anything, or what," she adds in, trying to defuse the bomb she doesn't know she's just lit. "I just heard him say that after that meeting, he could be headed back to California."

I turn to the man at the end of the boat, my heart beating in my stomach and up to my throat.

He came all this way home, not just for his brother's wedding. Not just to see his family. Not to see me. He came this way for some business venture, one that would mean serving up the last meaningful slice of land in our beloved hometown to the one man who will swallow it whole.

I don't even recognize him.

I can feel the heat radiating off of Luna. As Derrick turns the boat back in the direction of the docks, she stands slowly.

"So, you came back to sell off my mountain, there, Hunter?" she calls. Everyone on the boat grows quiet. He looks from her to Derrick, then his eyes land on me. And I make sure, no matter how much I want to, that my gaze doesn't falter from his. I want him to feel me.

He swallows and looks back up to her.

"Luna, that's not exactly—" he starts to say just as Derrick revs the engine in reverse to slow us down as we cruise in toward the boat slip. We all hop up to grab bumpers and ropes, and as we tie it off, Luna stands perfectly still in the center of the boat.

Shane stands slowly and walks toward her.

"Maybe we can talk about this—"

But Luna turns on her heel, her black locks flicking him in the face as she rushes off the boat and up the stairs. The rest of the crew slowly gathers their things, and Derrick helps Ryder, Mila, and Annabelle off. Kaylee slips off behind us so that the only two left on the boat are me and my ex-best friend.

He's staring at me.

"Jules, this isn't—"

"Are you meeting with Reed Miller while you're here?" I cut him off. I stand slowly so that we're facing each other dead-on.

"Yes."

I nod my head slowly, my eyes drifting up to the sky. I get off the boat and start walking toward the steps when he calls my name. I keep walking, but he calls my name again.

I freeze and turn back to him, and the sight of him at the end of the dock almost brings me to my knees. He's a little scruffier than he used to be, a little more of a man. But there's that same gleam in his eyes that was there back when my whole world revolved around him. And for this one moment, I realize it revolves around him again.

"I'm not just gonna leave like this," he says. I narrow my eyes on his, looking for whatever bit of my friend is left in there—but I think he went to California years ago and never came back.

"Why not? Nothing you haven't done before."

I watch as his whole face sinks, and I hate how much guilt I feel for causing him any sort of pain or disappointment. But I turn and walk up the stairs, back to my car, and back to that time in limbo, in between these two versions of Shane.

9

FALL OF JUNIOR YEAR

This has been the absolute longest day ever, and it's only second period. Not a good sign. Mom was out all night again, and I know from experience that if she's not home before I leave for school, it's not gonna be fun when I get home.

"Yoo-hoo, Earth to Jules," I hear Tommy's sing-song voice say from behind me as he reaches a hand around to wave in my face. I shake my head and smile, clearing the constant worry that is my mother from my head and turning to him.

"Hey, morning," I say. I look forward to this class every day. Not because I have an overwhelming love for history, but because Tommy sits behind me, and Shane sits next to me. And, like always, about nine seconds before the bell, our best friend walks in, cool as a cucumber, like the world is on his time.

"Lucky break, Mr. Hunter," Mrs. Clayborne says as she closes the classroom door and heads to the front of the room.

"What's up?" Shane says as he slides into his chair.

Everyone else nods and says their hellos, and Tommy and I just wait around for it to be our turn. Shane is the swim god at Meade High, and we know it. Tommy basks in the glory of being the big man on campus's best bud. Me? I'm just along for the ride. I don't flourish in the spotlight like Tommy does, but this last year has also been one of the best of my life for a number of reasons, the primary one being Shane.

Finally, he turns to me and hits me with that grin that lights up my whole damn world. Shane has quickly become something I've never had in my life over the last year or so. Luna is always there. She has been since first grade. But she's got a lot on her own plate and a very serious boyfriend whom she typically comes attached to. Kirby is my rock. She knows all the ins and outs of my life, but she has her own issues. My uncle died when we were kids, and my Aunt Ruby has been scrambling to keep a roof over their heads ever since, so Kirby works a lot to help out. They have their own demons to deal with—too many for my mom to be one.

Tommy is the fun friend. The friend you look for when you need distractions. When you want to smile, to laugh, to forget about anything else.

But Shane is something more. He's a combination of all of those. He's funny; he's dependable. But he's also everything I'm not. We make up for each other's flaws; we grow with each other. He's my calm. He's that strange, peaceful silence on a winter night when the world is asleep, just waiting to be blanketed.

"Morning, sunshine," he says to me as he shakes his coat off.

"Morning," I say. "Glad you could join us," I add

sarcastically. He shoots me another one of those shit-eating grins.

"Anything for the people," he says. Tommy ruffles his hair and sits back in his chair.

"I'm so fucking glad it's finally Friday," Tommy says. We wait for the plans to come, but instead, Tommy growls. "Ah, damn. Forgot I have a shift at Happy's tonight."

"Ah, man," Shane says. "What about you, Jules?"

I shrug.

"I'm free." He nods.

"Cool. I can come pick you up after practice," he says. I nod and turn to the front of the room where Mrs. Clayborne has her hand on her hip, waiting for us to be done with our own conversation so she can start class.

While she starts to go on about the Cold War, my mind is already skipping eight hours ahead to when Shane and I will be together, alone. It doesn't happen a lot; me, Tommy, and Shane normally come as a pack of three. But every once in a while, there's a break, and it's just us. Those are some of my favorite times.

The rest of the day goes by as painfully slow as the first part of it did, until I'm finally home, changing into some comfy yoga pants and Tommy's hoodie that I stole a few weeks back. My phone buzzes on my bed.

Your chariot awaits, he says. I smile.

Be right there.

I walk to the front door but pause at the mirror on the wall to check myself one more time. There are faded circles underneath my brown eyes from too many consecutive nights of covering my mom's shifts at the bakery, working at the cafe, and then staying up late to finish my homework.

My auburn hair hangs well below my shoulders; the only thing giving it any life is the natural wave it has to it. My freckles have almost all disappeared with the summer, and I'm starting to look like the winter version of myself.

I turn and walk out the side door, down the porch steps to his truck, and slide in.

"What's up?" he says, dumping what's left in a bag of popcorn into his mouth. I swear, he eats his weight in calories every day and never gains a pound. He reaches over the armrest and hands me a hot chocolate from Barb's, the little gas station/convenience store on the edge of town. This hot chocolate is to die for. The best there is, I'm convinced, and they only sell it when it starts to get cool out.

"No way! It's cocoa season!" I say, licking my lips as I pull the plastic tab back to take a sweltering sip. He laughs.

"You're gonna burn your tongue off," he says, whipping the truck around and pulling out of my driveway.

"Worth it," I tell him with a shrug. With every turn of the tires in any direction that is away from my house, I feel lighter and lighter.

"So, what are we doing?" he asks me, reaching a hand over toward me. I shoot him a look.

"You think I'm sharing my first Barb's hot chocolate of the season with you?" I ask. He lifts an eyebrow, his eyes never leaving the road. His lips turn up into a mischievous smile.

"Yes," he says simply.

"What on earth makes you think that?"

"Because you can't resist when I go like this." He

proceeds to stick out his bottom lip in the most perfect pout I've ever seen, and I laugh and shake my head.

"Here," I say, sticking the cup out to him. He chuckles, and he takes it and takes a sip, and there are butterflies in my stomach when I think of the fact that his lips have now been where mine once were. He hands it back to me, and I take another sip, looking out the window at the red and gold that is starting to take over the trees.

"Always have my back," he says with a laugh. I smile and turn back to him.

"Always," I say with more seriousness in my voice than I intended for. Our eyes meet for a brief moment, and he nods, and for something unsaid, it was incredibly loud.

We drive a little farther, and he pulls into the state park that sits at the center of the lake. There are paths, trails, playgrounds, and a public beach. But the locals know there are also some secret trails that lead down to the water, and that's exactly where we're headed. He gets out and walks around the truck to wait for me. I bend over to gather my hair into another unruly nest on the top of my head, but when I pop back up, his eyes are scanning me.

"What?" I ask.

"Is that Tommy's?" he asks. I look down at the oversized hoodie I'm wearing and nod.

"Yeah. I took it the last time we were all at your house." He nods for a moment then leads me up to the path we've taken before. At the edge of the water, there's a single wooden bench that has definitely seen better days. This part of the lake is unkempt and untouched by the park keepers. Tall grass grows around the clearing, and the path is more overgrown each time we take it. But that's why we come here. Because no one else does.

He plops down on the end of the bench, and I sit down next to him, pulling my legs up underneath me as I look out over the water. I sip on my hot chocolate a little more and lean back.

"I got another call today," he says, now digging through a bag of trail mix to pluck out only the raisins. Yes, he only eats the raisins. Like a goddamn psycho. I perk up and look at him.

"From another coach?" I ask. He nods. He's been getting what feels like a call a week from another college coach who is interested in talking to him. His parents have slammed his spring schedule with college visits galore so he can start to narrow down his decision. "Which one?"

"Georgia," he says. I nod.

"That's great!" I say, reaching a hand toward his bag and grabbing a handful.

"Have you thought any more about school?" he asks. I clap the crumbs off my hands and turn to face him.

"Not really," I say. "I mean, I think about it a lot. But I worry about her."

His grayish eyes flick up to me, and his expression is completely serious.

"Your mom?" he asks. I nod. "What about her?"

I sigh and let my eyes trail off past him and into the mountains.

"A lot of things. I worry that if I leave, and she ends up in a ditch somewhere, no one will know." I drop my eyes to the ground. "I think about her up here, the biggest hazard to her own safety being herself. If I'm not there to protect her from *her*, who will be?"

He nods and lets out a long breath, shifting on the bench. I can hear the leaves crunching beneath his boots.

"Jules, can I tell you something?" Our eyes meet again, and I feel my pulse quicken. "This whole thing with your mom, and her drinking, and you having to take care of her...it's not right, Jules."

I feel myself locking up, shutting down. I turn away from him, looking back over the water, crossing my arms over my body. The same way my body reacts anytime anything about my mom comes up. When teachers have asked if she'll be at conferences or back-to-school nights. When my friends ask if she'll care if we stay at Ryder's for the weekend. When my aunt or Kirby asks me when the last time I saw her was.

The answers are too hard, too depressing to give. Because the answer, in every single one of those circumstances, is that she loves something else more than she loves me. Or at least, that's what it feels like. I know that's not the truth. I know she's sick. But I'm just tired —exhausted—from being her caretaker.

"Jules," he says, his voice soft. "Look at me. Don't turn away."

I close my eyes and draw in another sharp breath. I feel his hand on my arm, and he gently tugs to spin me toward him.

"Jules. Don't turn away," he whispers. I finally look up at him. "I know I don't have to tell you. I know you know it's fucked up. But let's, for one sec, pretend like that's not the case. If you could go anywhere after next year, where would you want to go?"

I think for a moment.

"California."

He tilts his head and the corner of his mouth pulls up.

"Really? Why California?"

"Because it's the exact opposite of here," I say with a shrug. "I mean, I do love it here. But no harsh winters. No drunk mom. Sounds nice," I say with a sad smile. He grins back.

"Alright, then. California it is," he says, leaning back against the wood of the bench and draping his arm behind me.

"What?"

"Well, I'm getting scouted by USC, and you know they already offered me a scholarship. I can accept it whenever I want. You apply there, and once you get in, I'll do it."

My eyes widen.

"What?" I ask again. "Do you...do you even want to go there?"

He chuckles and shrugs.

"I mean, why not? I want to go to a lot of places, but we have plenty of time for that when we're old, right?" His use of "we" has my mind jumping back and forth like a ping-pong ball.

"We" as in us? Together?

"But you haven't even been out there yet. Or to any of the other schools you got offers from. How do you know you won't want to go somewhere else?"

"Well, are you going somewhere else?" he asks. I bite my bottom lip and sit back. His eyes drop down to his hands for a minute. "I wanna be where you are, Jules." My heart makes my whole chest rattle. *I want to be where you are, too.* "You're my best friend."

"Hey, hey, now," a voice behind us says, making us jump. "Making plans without me?"

Tommy emerges from the edge of the trail, holding an energy drink in one hand and a fast food bag in the other.

"Tom, hey," Shane says. "I thought you were working?"

"They messed up the schedule," he says, "so I'm not in till tomorrow. You guys makin' college plans?"

I swallow and look to Shane. He clears his throat.

"We're just talking," he says. "Just trying to figure out where it is we want to, uh, go. You think you're gonna go away, Tom?"

A slow, sad smile tugs at Tommy's normally playful mouth, his gaze shifting from Shane to me. Then he shakes his head.

"I think you both know the answer to that," he says. Shane's eyes drop to the ground. Tommy walks around to the front of the bench, putting his stuff down and turning around. "Let's not beat around the bush. I've known my whole life I was a Meade Lake lifer."

His eyes jump across the tops of the mountains, scanning that sunset we've all seen so many times.

"Tommy, you could…" I start to say, but not sure where I'm going with it. Tommy's not exactly an A-plus student. He's not exactly a C-plus student, either. I've stayed up writing more papers for him than I care to admit, just to make sure he moved on to junior year with us. Tommy's got a heart of gold, and he makes the people he cares about a priority in his life. He makes having fun a priority in his life. He makes a lot of things a priority; schoolwork is just not one of them.

He shakes his head in my direction and smiles again.

"Come on, guys," he says with a wave of his hand. "I think we all knew from the start I'd be hangin' around here for the rest of my days. Plowing the roads like my pops."

Shane and I fall silent again, unsure of what to say. Because even though we see him for so much more, he's probably right.

"So, where are you guys headed?" Tommy asks, breaking the awkward silence for us.

Shane looks to me then to Tommy.

"We were thinking California."

I look at Tommy, bracing for his reaction that his two best friends were just plotting to move over three thousand miles from him.

But finally, he nods.

"California," Tommy says quietly. "Well, go. Go off and do amazing things. Get a nice place with a nice couch where I can crash with the California babes I meet whenever I come to visit."

We laugh, and I get up from the bench and walk toward him, throwing my arms around his neck.

"Make me proud," he says, just above a whisper.

WE SIT by the water for a few more hours, laughing, and talking, and eating the never-ending supply of junk food that comes with the territory of hanging out with two teenage boys all the time. Finally, as the last bit of daylight is zapped up, Shane stands.

"Should we get outta here?" he asks. I nod and stand up, wrapping my arms around my body. Guess it's time to see what sort of shape my mother is in tonight.

We say our goodbyes to Tommy then head back to

Shane's truck. The car ride is quiet, but I've come to appreciate the casual quiet that comes from being with Shane. No pressure, no awkward tension when the air isn't filled up by conversation. When he pulls into my driveway, I let out a long breath.

"Are you good?" he asks. "You want me to come in with you?"

I look up at him with round eyes, eyes that are pleading for him to do just that. But I shake my head.

"Nah, I'm good," I tell him. He nods as I grab my bag and open the door. "See you tomorrow?"

He nods as I close the door.

"Oh, wait, Jules," I hear him say, and I turn back. He opens his door and walks toward me, something in his hand. "Here."

I look down at the giant, navy, Meade Lake Swimming sweatshirt in his hands.

"What's this?" I ask him.

"My hoodie," he says. I tilt my head, a little confused. "I want you to steal my hoodies, too."

I take the sweatshirt from his hand, looking at the fabric.

"Actually," he says, "I want you to steal mine *instead*."

I don't know what to say, because I'm not sure what any of this means. I know that I've become codependent on Shane over the last year. I know that my days are better with him in it. But I never, under no circumstances, assumed that he felt the same way. Watching your parents' love story crash and burn into flames fueled by Jack Daniels will do that to you. It'll make you think that loving someone, letting someone mean that much, can only end in a fiery crash and burn.

I won't lose Shane that way. I can't. So we'll stay like this, safe in our best-friend bubble.

At least, that's what I thought, until right now.

Our eyes are locked on each other, and I can tell he's nervous—something that Shane Hunter very seldom is. He commands every room he walks into, every pool he dives into. But right now, he looks out of control.

I set my bag down and reach down to the hem of Tommy's sweatshirt, pulling it up over my head. I slip Shane's over, and pull it down, letting the fabric that smells of him swim around me, clinging to my body. My eyes lock on his again, and I smile.

Then I turn on my heel and walk up the steps and into my house.

10

"**I**s he coming?" I ask, holding the phone between my ear and my shoulder as I shovel an overdue load of laundry into the dryer.

"I'm not sure," Luna says.

"Well, then I'm not going," I tell her.

"We're going," she says matter-of-factly.

"Luna, why would you want to go? Risk seeing him again?" I ask her.

"Because I'm not going to let him stop *me* from seeing *my* friends," she says, and I can practically hear her put her hands on her hips through the phone line. "He doesn't have that power over us."

I pause for a moment.

Does he? Does he still have power over me?

I shake my head.

No. No, he does not.

"Fine. I'll pick you up at eight. But bring those chocolate-covered pretzels you brought last time."

She scoffs.

"Fine. See you at eight," she says.

When Ryder and Mila put the invite out, they didn't mention Shane's name, but that could be purposeful. See, my friends have one downfall, and that is that they're friends with *everyone*. Some loyalty.

I can't really blame them, though, for not feeling a need to close Shane off like I do. He didn't abandon them—at least, not in the same way he did to me.

They were all close.

But no one was as close as Shane and I were.

I shiver at the memory of curling up in a ball on my bedroom floor, clutching my favorite photo of us, wondering how the fuck I could have meant so little to him. But I shake it off and walk over to my closet, pulling out the tightest pair of jeans I own and a blouse that fits a little more snugly than some of my others.

I give my hair a few strokes with a brush, give my eyelashes a few flicks of mascara, and I'm out.

"Why do you look hot?" Luna asks as she gets in the car. "When did we decide to look hot?"

I want to shove her. She should be a supermodel in her own right, whether or not she's wearing yoga pants and furry boots.

"Wait. Are you hot for *him?*" she asks. "Did you get hot for *him?*"

I roll my eyes.

"No, Luna. I did not get hot for *him,*" I lie. "Nothing I do is for him, or ever will be again."

Luna laughs as she turns to look out the window.

"Hell hath no fury like a woman scorned."

· · ·

WE PULL into Ryder's driveway, and my stomach does a little flip. I see all the cars I recognize, and then one I don't: a BMW that I can only assume is Shane's rental. I sigh and follow Luna around the back to the patio.

"Hey, hey!" Derrick says as we walk down the stone path.

"Look what the cat dragged in!" Mila says, standing to greet us and holding her hand out to the empty chairs around the fire. "We have tacos inside, drinks by the bar, and s'mores here."

"Thanks," Luna says as we give the rest of our hugs and kisses. When we get to Shane on the other side of the fire, we both turn away. After everyone gets their food and drinks, they take their seats around the fire. I sit down, my plate in my lap, but realize I forgot to get a drink. I hop back up and walk toward the bar, only to find myself feet away from Shane. He sticks his hand into the cooler and pulls out a water, sliding it across the bar to me. With a quick nod, he returns to his chair next to Ryder and Derrick, and I'm left dumbfounded again at the details that he's carried with him all these years.

"So, Shane, what is California like?" Ryder asks after a few minutes of small talk. The group grows quiet, everyone anxiously awaiting his response. He clears his throat, shifting in his seat. But despite everything, he's still not awkward. He still commands all eyes on him. Even mine.

"California is amazing," he says with an honest shrug. "It's everything Meade Lake's not. Warm, sunny all the time."

My eyes meet his, shooting daggers into him as he talks.

The exact opposite of here.

"It's funny, though. Being back here makes me realize how much I loved growing up here. There's nothing quite like this place."

His eyes find me when he says it, and I clear my throat.

"But come on, the California beaches? The California ladies?" Ryder says, and Mila playfully pinches his arm.

Everyone chuckles, and Shane slowly lifts his eyes to me again.

"It's got a lot of perks," he says. "But, like I said, it's no Meade Lake. Always sort of feels like something's missing, ya know?"

I'm seething in my chair, my eyes narrowed in on him.

"Yeah, well, it sure wasn't missing enough for you to stay for ten, eleven years now, was it?" I ask. My eyes widen when I realize I asked it out loud, and I stand slowly from my chair. Luna goes to stand, but I hold my hand out, letting her know I need a minute to myself.

I follow the path down to the docks and walk across the wood, my feet pounding on it in unison with my heart. I cross my arms and sit at the very edge, letting the freezing fall air ground me.

I was wrong.

It still hurts as much as it did eleven years ago.

The wounds have been reopened. And now I need him gone.

I hear footsteps coming down the dock, and I close my eyes. I don't want him to check on me. I don't want him near me. I want him 3,000 miles away, where he's supposed to be.

"Jules?" I hear Derrick's voice ask, and I perk up and

turn around to see him, Ryder, and Luna all looking down at me. Ryder's holding onto the railing that Derrick installed for him after his sight went, but his eyes are right on me.

"I'm sorry, guys," I say, immediately filled with shame. "I don't know what's getting into me. I guess I thought I was over everything after all these years, but seeing him…I don't know."

Derrick sits on one side of me, and Luna sits on the other. Ryder stands near us.

"None of us know every single detail of what happened on the ice that night," Luna says, taking my hand. "But I think we would have had to have been idiots to not know how much Shane meant to you."

"Yeah. He was your, uh–" Derrick starts.

"Your best friend," Ryder says. "And we realize you have some unfinished business. Maybe some things to say."

I shrug out of Luna's grasp and flip my hair over one shoulder.

"That's just it, though. I don't want to finish any business, anymore. We had eleven years for that. And instead, I spent those years moving on with my life. I just want to keep moving on. And then he comes back and tries to sell off Luna's land?"

Luna swallows and looks down into the water, guilt in her eyes.

"What?" I ask.

"Well, uh, I talked to him up at the house. That's not exactly what's happening."

I look from her to Derrick to Ryder.

"What do you mean?"

"Well, uh, it sounds like his boss makes all the

purchasing decisions. He had his eye on this land for a long time, and when Shane told him he was coming home for Ty's wedding, he asked him to scope it out. Shane's working with Reed Miller to try and look at some other options to present to his boss. So as much as it sucks, it's not really Shane's fault," Luna says.

I swallow and look out to the lake.

"Look, Jules. We know you have history. But Shane hasn't really...changed all that much, ya know? He might be around for a while to negotiate this deal. Maybe you could try talking to him again, ya know?" Ryder says.

"Yeah. I think the Shane that's back here is the same guy that was here all those years ago," Luna says.

That's exactly what I am afraid of.

11

_____

WINTER OF JUNIOR YEAR

"**D**o you ever get sick of winning?" Tommy asks Shane as we drop our stuff down on Shane's couch and lunge for the carryout we grabbed.

Shane laughs as he grabs three waters from the fridge and walks over to the living room. I shimmy my snow-covered boots off and jump onto the couch. It's been snowing for hours, and it's not supposed to stop anytime soon. The Hunters got out of town before the snow started, and with Ty away at school, it's a free house for all of us.

"Seriously, my man. You're a fucking legend," Tommy says, then he nudges me. "Am I right, Jules?"

I look at him, then I look at Shane and roll my eyes.

"Okay, okay. Let's not give him _too_ big of a head," I say with a sheepish smile. Shane chucks a pillow at me. Just as I'm shoving a slice of pizza in my mouth, the front door bursts open, and in comes the crew, shaking the snow off themselves and stripping out of all their winter clothes in the foyer.

"Hey, hey, watch the hardwoods," Shane calls playfully as he walks over to greet them. Luna and Daniel are attached as the lips per usual, barely letting go of each other to walk through the door. Derrick and Ryder are laughing and rumbling through the house, and my heart is full. These people are *my* people. I snuggle back into the couch and finish my pizza, chatting with Luna as Daniel clutches onto her hand while he pretends to listen to the guys talk about the latest Steelers game.

"Alright, alright, people," Tommy says, finally doing what he does best, becoming

the center of attention. "Seeing as we're all gonna be here all night, how about a game of football?"

Everyone perks up, and I laugh and shake my head as they make their way back to the door to put back on their layers. I let them all get there first and follow behind, slowly wrapping my scarf around my head.

"Don't forget a hat," Shane says from behind me, resting his chin on my shoulder for the briefest of moments before tossing me my beanie.

"Thanks," I tell him. He waits for me at the door and closes it behind me. He throws his arm around my shoulder.

"So," he says, and my heart picks up its pace. "You ready to get your ass kicked?" He gives me a gentle push, sending me stumbling into a pile of snow. He stands in front of me, lips curled into that devilish smile while I gather myself and get back on my feet.

"Oh, it's *on*, motherfucker!" I scream, chasing him down the hill. He stops just before the edge of the frozen water, turning and catching me by surprise. He throws me over his shoulder and runs onto the ice where the rest of the crew is already picking teams.

"We get Jules!" Luna says.

"Fine. We get Shane, then," Tommy says. "Even though he's not really much of an athlete." Shane shoves him, and they tackle each other.

"Alright, alright! Stop it before you crack the damn ice. Let's get this rolling!" Luna says, ever the mom of the group.

We get down into stance just as Tommy is calling the play.

I'm directly across from Shane, who makes eyes at me, pointing his fingers to his eyes then to me. I laugh and bite my lip, wanting that sensation of his hands on me again but fighting it with all my might.

You can't want him, Jules. You can't.

"Down. Set. Hike!" Tommy calls, passing the ball off to Ryder, who has no problem busting through us to score in one quick move.

"Fuck yes!" Tommy calls, thrusting his fist into the air. We all laugh and shake our heads, except for Luna. Luna doesn't like to lose.

Her eyes gloss over with that competitive nature she has as she bends down to call the play.

"Down, set, hike!" she yells. I blow past Shane, turning to look for the ball, and just as it flies through the air toward me, I feel hands on me, then I feel myself losing footing. We go crashing to the ice, and then I feel a sharp pain on the side of my head.

"Jesus, Jules!" Shane yells. When I open my eyes, I'm caged into his arms, as if he were trying to break my fall. "I'm sorry! Are you okay?"

I shake my head and steady myself.

"Yeah, yeah," I say. "I think…" I reach my hand up to my head and feel warmth, and I stop. It comes down covered in blood.

"Aw, shit. I'm so sorry. I slipped. I tried to catch us. Let's go get you a bandage," he says, pulling me up from the ice. "I'm taking her in, guys. You can keep playing."

"You okay, Jules? You want me to come?" Luna asks. I shake my head.

"No, no. Just win the damn game, would ya?" I ask. She winks in my direction and turns back.

Shane leads me off the ice and up the yard, keeping his arm around my back the whole way. He leads me in through the basement door and sits me up on the edge of the pool table in the Hunters' huge rec room.

"Be right back," he says, heading for the bathroom. He emerges with a first-aid kit and starts rummaging through. As he examines the cut on the side of my head, I examine him. Every inch of his perfectly cut face. He looks so much like Mrs. Hunter, who definitely could have been a model in her earlier years—shit, she could be one now. Bronzed skin, no matter what season, with those grayish-blue eyes that just tear me the hell open every time they look at me. Perfectly rounded lips, square jaw that melts me.

He really is perfect.

But you can't, Jules. You can't love him, because then you'll lose him.

He dabs at my head with a cloth then squeezes some antibiotic ointment on it and covers it with a large bandage as gently as possible.

"I'm sorry again, Jules," he says, closing up the kit and sliding it down the pool table.

"Stop apologizing," I tell him. "It's part of the game."

"I know, I know," he says. "I just hate that I hurt

you." His face is twisted into a painful scowl, like he's replaying everything that just happened out on that ice.

He lifts his eyes to mine, and I swallow. I remember what he said about his dad—his real dad—and I realize that's where this is coming from.

He and I are so much alike in that way. Trying like hell to fight our destiny.

"You could never hurt me, Shane."

He steps a little bit closer, forcing my legs to part some so he can stand flush against the pool table. I can smell that same scent that cradles me to sleep every night that I sleep in his hoodie, and it drives me a little wild.

"No one should ever hurt you," he whispers, reaching up to tuck a piece of my hair behind my ear. He reaches his other hand up and cups my chin, and suddenly, I feel like I've lost all control. Like whatever move I make next, I cannot be held accountable for.

He bends down slightly so that our faces are just inches apart when my phone vibrates in my pocket, making us both jump. I look up at him, but we both know I have to check it. Everyone else that I would talk to is here at this house. So, there's only one person it could be, and that's Kirby.

"Kirb?" I ask. "Everything okay?"

"Where are you?" she asks, her voice traced with panic, which is completely uncharacteristic of her.

"Shane's," I say, sliding off the table. "What's going on?"

"Officer Trout just called my mom," she breathes into the phone. "Your mom got into an accident."

I feel queasy, and I sink back against the table. Shane

reaches out to steady me, his eyes pleading to know what's going on.

"Is she…"

"She's alive," Kirby says. "She's actually mostly okay, just a broken wrist. But her blood alcohol levels…she's in some trouble now, Jules. She almost hit another car."

"Oh, God," I whisper, my lip trembling. "What do I…where do I…"

"She'll need to spend the night in the hospital tonight," Kirby says. "And my mom will bring her home in the morning. I'm sorry, Jules. Love you."

I hang up without another word.

"I…I think I need to go home," I tell Shane.

"What's going on, Jules? Is she okay?" he asks. I turn to him, and then, like a wave, the tears flow from my eyes. He pulls me into his chest, cradling my head in his hand as he rests his cheek on top of it. And for what feels like forever, he just lets me cry, like he's had to do so much over the course of our friendship.

"She's okay," I finally whisper. "But I think she really fucked up this time. I just want to go home, okay? Can I borrow your truck?"

"Jules…" Shane starts to say, looking out toward the window. "Jules, we can't leave right now. It's the biggest storm we've had in years. Even my truck won't get up that mountain right now."

I stare out the sliding glass door, and I know he's right.

"How about I get you set up in my room?" he asks. "I'll tell the rest of the guys you're not feeling great from your fall, and then when they're all settled, I'll come back. I mean, if that's okay?" I nod and follow him up both flights of stairs.

When we get to his room, I take it all in, this space that just feels like him. In the year that we've been friends, I haven't been up here yet. Normally, we all crash on couches in the living room and basement, wherever we drop. I sit on the edge of his bed and wait as he digs through his drawers for a t-shirt and some pajama pants.

"These are the closest things I have to what might fit you," he says with a smile. I force a smile back and thank him. "You can change in the bathroom. I'll be up soon, okay?"

"No, no. Don't leave them," I tell him. But he shoots me a look, and we both know where he's going to be.

And just like that, Shane Hunter makes me feel like the most important person in the world again.

After he goes back downstairs, I strip down and slip into his pajamas, and there's something so sensual about his clothes touching me everywhere. I slip under the red comforter on his bed and curl up on his pillow, wondering which side he sleeps on normally. But before I can get too comfortable, the door opens, and he's back.

"Shane—"

But he holds his hand up.

"Before you start," he says, "Tommy is already passed out on the couch. Luna and Daniel are down in the guest room, doing God knows what. And Derrick and Ryder are still outside, tossing the ball around. Everyone is good."

He walks over toward his dresser and swiftly tugs his t-shirt up over his head, exposing that back that's been chiseled by years of discipline, years of laps and lifting weights to become the best version of him he could be. And if you ask me, he's done a pretty decent job of it.

He pulls a clean shirt out of the dresser and pulls it over his head then hops onto the bed and grabs the remote off the end table.

"So are we gonna talk about it?" he asks, sinking down so that we're almost nose to nose now. And just like that, the tears are back. It's like they know it's safe. They know *he's* safe. "Aw, Jules." He pulls me into him tighter.

"Why doesn't she want to do better for me?" I sob. "How do I make her want to stay alive?"

He doesn't answer me, because there's no answer to that question. Instead, he just lets me cry more while he holds me tighter than I've ever been held.

I WAKE up the next morning, hearing yelling from a level below. I startle awake, finding myself alone in Shane's bed. I scramble to pull on his hoodie and walk out the bedroom door. The morning light from the huge A-frame windows blinds me as I walk toward the steps, but I freeze when I hear a woman's voice from below.

Mrs. Hunter's voice.

"And *what* is she doing in your bed, Shane? I thought you were just friends," she says.

"Ma, we are just friends. She...she had a really shitty night, okay?"

"What kind of shitty night? What are you talking about?" I know I need to rescue him. This isn't his battle to fight or his story to tell, and I know he won't betray me.

"My mom got into an accident," I say from the bottom of the steps. Mrs. Hunter whips her head in my direction.

"What kind of accident? Is she alright?" she asks. I nod.

"She's okay. But I think after this, she's going to be in some, uh, legal trouble, Mrs. Hunter."

Mrs. Hunter is a strong woman. She's a go-getter; she's determined; she's no bullshit. And even though she and Dr. Hunter have their fun, she's still a mom. She loves her boys fiercely. I see her face soften as she tilts her head.

"Come here, Jules," she says. I look at Shane then do what she says. When I get to her, she wraps her arms around me and hugs me tight. "It's gonna be okay, sweetie. Shane, get the rest of your friends up here for breakfast. Once they go, we'll talk through this stuff with your mom and see what we can do, okay?"

I nod as she squeezes my hand.

The rest of the group makes their way groggily up the stairs, everyone looking equal parts shocked and concerned that the Hunters are home.

"Apparently, Mom and Dad didn't want to leave me alone in a storm this big," Shane says from the sunroom where Mrs. Hunter has spread out nothing less than a feast. "So they came home early this morning, as soon as the roads were safe."

I nod and snag a bagel from the platter in front of me. Shane nudges me under the table, and I look at him.

"Remember what she said. It's gonna be okay."

AFTER BREAKFAST, everyone gets their stuff together and heads out.

"Mrs. H, lovely spread, as usual," Tommy calls as he makes his way back out to his car.

"Thanks, Tommy," she says with a smile, closing the door behind him. She turns to Shane and me and nods toward the living room, where Dr. Hunter joins us. "So, tell us what happened."

I don't know what it is about the Hunters that makes it feel like such a safe space, but I quickly realize that Shane gets that quality from his parents. And whatever it is makes me open up like a damn book. I tell them everything, starting with my dad leaving to my mom's accident last night. And it doesn't feel scary or suffocating. It feels freeing, like I let a load off.

Dr. and Mrs. Hunter both nod as I talk, and when I finish, she reaches forward to squeeze my hand.

"My goodness," she finally says after shaking her head a few times. "That is quite a lot for a sixteen-year-old to carry around."

I nod slowly and shrug.

"Well, listen. We have a friend that's an attorney, so we'll give him a call this afternoon to see what your mom's options might be. His firm accepts a certain number of pro bono cases per year, so it might even be possible for them to represent her."

I feel another weight melt off my shoulders.

"And I have some friends who work in our chemical dependency unit at the hospital," Dr. Hunter chimes in. "Let me give them a call this afternoon and see if they have any tips, okay?"

I bite my lip to keep it from trembling and nod just as Mrs. Hunter stands and walks toward me. She cups my face in her hands and stares into my eyes.

"Look at me, honey," she says, and I do. "Hear me.

Hear what I'm about to say. I know she's your mother and you love her. But if she can't get the help she needs, you have to remember that you deserve so much more than that, okay? You are *worth* so much more. And I know my boy thinks so, too." She winks. My eyes float across the room to Shane. He's sitting on the edge of the couch, his hands clasped between his knees, and he doesn't even flinch when she says it. He doesn't look embarrassed or annoyed. He looks like it's true.

12

It's been a slow couple of weeks now that we're getting closer and closer to winter. After the summer crowd leaves, our events slow down a lot around here. Skiing and snow tubing pick up, and the resort is flocked by late November. But that little lag in between the last of the boats coming off the water and the first snowfall is the quietest time of year in Meade Lake. And it also happens to be my absolute favorite time of year here.

I baked a few batches of our seasonal cookies that we sell at a few of the shops in town that I'll deliver later today, and I'm icing them in pretty fall colors, getting as artistic as my decorating tools will let me.

It sounds silly to say that I actually have a passion for this. Baked goods. But it's so much more than that. Cakes, cookies, pastries, whatever it is, they bring people joy. Weddings, birthday parties, anniversaries. I love knowing that what I create here in the back of Marge's shop makes people gasp. That they really grasp a person's likes, personalities. That I'm able to turn that into something that they will remember.

I know some of my friends are business owners. Some people from high school went off to law school, some went off and became doctors.

Some went across the country and lived out a dream I thought I had.

But it turns out, I'm happy here. And I'm happy in this little shop, baking these cakes and cookies and cupcakes that will be with people on the best days of their lives.

The bell above the door chimes, and I clap the flour off my hands and walk to the front. Marge is off again today, says she's not feeling well. That's been happening a few times a week now, but I'm doing my best to ignore it and pretend it's nothing.

"Welcome to Marge's," I say, taking off my apron and looking up to greet whoever just walked in.

"It's been too damn long," Molly Hunter says, and I freeze. She hasn't aged since we were kids, I swear. Her light-brown hair is styled a little differently, in a chic cut that lands just above her shoulders. She has a few more crow's feet around her brown eyes, but I swear, that's it. Otherwise, she might as well have frozen in time.

"Mrs. Hunter," I say, breathy, completely thrown off. Just as I'm walking around the counter, the bell chimes again, and Shane walks in behind her. Before I can react, she throws her arms around me, pulling me into her. She still wears the same perfume, one that probably costs more than a month's rent at my place. But it feels so good seeing her.

All these years, we've been mere miles apart, but I

could never bring myself to see her and Dr. Hunter. What would I say?

"I don't know why your son took off and abandoned me, but how have you been?"

I couldn't be there, in that house, with them.

Not that they've been around much, anyway, I'm sure.

They were hardly around when their sons were still living at home. I can't imagine they stick around here much these days with an empty house. I heard they bought a house in the Virgin Islands somewhere, too. I'm sure they've been spending plenty of time there over the years, especially since Dr. Hunter retired.

"My God, it's good to see you, girl," she says. "When this one told me he ran into you and that you worked here, I just *had* to come see you. I was so sorry I missed you at the wedding. Shane said it was so good to see you."

Our eyes lock on each other's for a moment before I turn away.

"It was...good to see Shane, too," I lie, as if he isn't just feet away from me.

She holds me at arm's length, looking me up and down, searching my eyes.

"You are just as gorgeous as ever," she says to me, and I feel fire rise in my cheeks. "Listen, I need to place an order for two dozen cupcakes. *Someone's* birthday is next week, ya know." She nods her head in Shane's direction, who is awkwardly standing with his hands shoved in his pockets, pretending to look at some of the bagged candies we have near the back.

Oh, shit. Shane's birthday. I'd be lying if I said I didn't think about it every year on the date and whispered a quick prayer that, wherever he was in the world, whatever he was doing, whoever he was with, it was a good day.

Because through it all, he deserved that.

"Ah, yes," I say, quickly shifting my eyes from Shane back to Mrs. Hunter.

"It's not every year I get to celebrate one of my son's birthdays with them in person. So, we're doing it big. A little shindig at the house. Are you still living with your mom?" she asks. It's not meant to be a dig; I know she understands why I stayed home so long. "How is she doing, by the way?"

"I, uh, I actually moved out a few months ago," I tell her. And then I smile. "She's doing well, actually."

Mrs. Hunter smiles back, tilting her head.

"You don't know how good it does my heart to hear that," she says. "Well, listen, write down your address here. I'm mailing invitations tomorrow."

I smile as I take her pen, jotting down my address. Only Molly Hunter would mail out invitations to her almost-thirty-year-old son's birthday party, two weeks before it's supposed to happen.

"You'll come, yes? We're inviting your whole crew. It's been so long since I've seen some of those faces. It'll be like homecoming!" she says, clapping her hands. I stammer a bit, desperately wishing I were witty enough to come up with some sort of excuse. But she caught me, cornered me. She pulls out her wallet and hands me a credit card. I walk back around the counter and ring her up.

"Oh, um, you didn't mention what you wanted on the cupcakes," I tell her, avoiding the question about his party. She takes her card back and waves a hand in my direction.

"Surprise us. You probably still know him better than anyone," she says with a laugh. "Check your mailbox soon! I can't wait to see you again, sweetie!" she calls as she walks out the door. Shane stands awkwardly by the door, his eyes on mine.

"Did my mom just invite you to my birthday party, like I'm a damn five-year-old?" he asks.

Then he chuckles, shaking his head. I can't help but smile, as much as I don't want to. "See ya, Jules."

THE NEXT MORNING, I'm pouring myself a cup of coffee in my kitchen while early-morning episodes of *The Golden Girls* fill the house with noise. I walk to the back door, which has a perfect view of the lake down below.

I know most of my friends live on the water in houses that would make even the richest man jealous. Not because they're all massive, but because of how close they are to the water. Because they can wake up, take a few steps, and have their toes in Meade Lake.

But up here, I can see it all. I can see the water, the mountains, the trees, the cars on the road. I can see it all from my little cabin up in the sky. I can take it all in without feeling like I'm drowning in it.

My slippers glide across the floor, my robe flowing behind me like I'm some sort of queen in her castle. But just as I reach the couch, I jump when there's a knock on my door. I look through the window at the top of the door, and I freeze when I realize it's him.

Panic sets in.

He hasn't seen me first thing in the morning in a

very, *very* long time. Back when I could wake up as dewy and perky and perfect as when my teenage self went to sleep. When it took no effort.

Now, it takes a little more caffeine to get that same pep in my step. It takes a little more concealer to hide these circles under my eyes. It takes a little more effort to look effortless.

I sigh.

It's too late now.

I pull the door open and stare at him over the edge of my mug as I draw in another sip of liquid energy.

"Mornin'," he says, holding up a foam cup with *Barb's* written across it in red writing. "I brought you a cup of Barb's hot cocoa, but it looks like you already got started."

I smile as I put my mug down by my side and take the cup from him.

"Thank you," I say. He really doesn't forget a damn thing. "What are you doing here?"

He smiles and pulls something out of the back pocket of his jeans that fit him way too nicely.

"Mom wanted me to hand-deliver this," he says, rubbing his temple. He hands over a blue envelope with my name written in calligraphy, and I almost laugh. "It's like she's making up for all those years of never being around. I can't believe I'm a grown man that just hand-delivered an invitation to my own birthday party because my mom made me." This time, I do laugh.

"Yeah, that's pretty pathetic," I tell him. He grins, and I melt a little.

"I also came by because I, uh...I wanted to talk to you," he says. I swallow, and every ounce of carelessness

I have left leaves my body. "I wanted to explain what I'm doing back here."

"You don't have to explain anything," I say. "You don't owe me."

His eyes find mine immediately, and the hurt behind them makes me look away. He sits on the porch step, and I pull the door closed behind me and do the same.

"I work for a company called Easton and Myers," he says. They buy and sell commercial and residential real estate all over the country."

I nod, peeling the plastic tab back and taking a sip of the best hot cocoa on the planet.

"I got put into the running about a month back for a promotion to regional manager," he says. "But there are two positions open. One back on the west coast, and one on the east coast. When I told my boss I was coming back here for my brother's wedding, he handed me a list of areas he wanted me to scope out. If I find some good deals, I can have my choice of which position I want."

I swallow.

"Like I said, with the exception of traveling to a few different sites now and then, the job is remote. So as long as I'm in the same time zone as the properties we're looking at, I can work from anywhere."

I nod again.

"And one of those properties was the mountain," I say. He nods, his eyes dropping to his hands that are folded between his knees.

"Yeah," he says. "I didn't even realize what property it was until I got here. But as soon as I did, I called up Reed Miller to see if there were any other comparable plots in the area. He's still doing some digging."

I nod again, and he turns his whole body to me.

"Jules, I know it's been a long, *long* time. But I would never do something like that. I would never sell Luna out—or any of you guys. I'm still me," he says. My eyes lift to his, and I so badly want to believe him. I see the teenage kid behind the grayish blue, pleading with me, asking me to trust him. I don't know how to respond, because I can't. So I just nod.

"With all that said, it looks like I will be around here for a little while," he says. "So I was really hoping that we could…"

I feel my body tense up, preparing to fight off whatever emotions are coming at me.

"We had fun, didn't we, Jules?" he asks. I turn to him and raise an eyebrow.

Before or after the ice?

I can't help but grin.

"Yeah, we did," I say.

"We have some catching up to do," he tells me. "What do ya say?"

I tilt my head.

"Did you just drive to my house, hand me an invitation to your birthday party, and ask me to be your friend?" I ask.

We both break out into laughter, and he shakes his head.

"Yeah," he says between chuckles, "I guess I did." I look down at the envelope in my hand, twirling it around in my fingers.

"I think I can do that," I say, despite all of the reasons that are screaming at me not to.

It's okay. I can be his friend. No harm in that.

Apparently, when Shane Hunter is back in town, there are no lies I won't tell myself.

13

FALL OF SENIOR YEAR

I roll out of bed and out to the kitchen, surprised when I don't see Mom lying on the couch, passed out from the night before. She wasn't home when I went to bed, which is never a good sign. I know she has a shift at the bakery today, and I set my alarm to be there in case she isn't.

The grace that Marge shows us doesn't go unnoticed. She knows my mom has a problem. She knows I'd do anything to solve it. And she knows how badly we need this money. I hate how much advantage she takes of Marge, especially because this job is so fun. I actually don't mind covering these shifts; there's something so peaceful and simultaneously exhilarating about the art that Marge makes in this kitchen. Mom was already let go from her job at the diner earlier this year—to be honest, I'm not even sure how she kept it as long as she did—and she's been struggling to find anything else nearby. Word travels fast through these hills, and people know who they can count on and who they can't. Unfortunately, no one knows better than me that Sherrie Grey is one who can't be counted on.

I pull into the parking lot at Marge's shortly before Mom's shift is about to start, tying my hair up in a bun and walking through to the back with haste, ready to see what we have for the day. But to my surprise, my mom pops up from behind the counter when I walk in.

"Morning, sweetie," she says. "What are you doing here?"

"I, uh…" I say, losing my train of thought. I can't remember the last time my mom was responsible. The last time she came through. It was probably a little less than a year ago, after the Hunters' lawyer friend helped her get probation in her DUI case. For a few weeks, she really tried. Made an effort. Made all her shifts, even made dinner a few nights a week. She was my mom again, for a little while.

And then reality set in and became too much to bear without a bottle by her side.

Marge comes around the corner and makes a face at me, shrugging as she walks by.

"You weren't home this morning, so I wasn't sure…" I say, not wanting to embarrass her. Her eyes drop to the ground.

"Honey, can we, uh…can we talk outside for a minute?" she asks. I swallow. This feels weird. Out of the norm. I nod and follow her outside.

She leans up against the brick of the building, pulling a cigarette out of her back pocket and lighting it —a habit I still loathe to my very core, but at least this one doesn't run the risk of her driving off the road and into the lake. One horrible vice at a time, I suppose. She draws in a long drag then leans her head back before she blows it out.

I keep my distance; one of my biggest fears has always been being the kid who wreaked of second-hand smoke in school. Mom has always been good about going outside to smoke, but I always worry that the smell will somehow attach itself to her and get to me.

"Well, I'll get right to it. It's not a secret that I've been sort of...well, a complete fucking trainwreck since your father left," she says. The bluntness of her statement takes me back, and I stare at her, blinking wildly.

That's the understatement of the year.

"The truth is, sweetie, I don't really know who I am without him. I've been with your father since I was sixteen years old. We grew up together. I became the woman I am while I was his," she says.

I cross my arms over my chest.

"The other night, though, I woke up in my car, parked on the side of Lake Shore Highway, up by the diner," she goes on, her bottom lip starting to tremble. "And I couldn't remember how I got there. And all I could think about was you. And how you deserve so much more than this, sweetie."

Her voice cracks, and I feel tears pricking at my own eyes.

"I owe it to you to be better. And I'm going to be," she says. "Starting right now. Your dad's not coming back. And I think it just took me this long to figure that out. I think I thought that if I stayed drunk, I would get through the months without him. But he's not coming back, and it's time for me to figure out who Sherrie is without Jedd. And that starts now."

She drops her cigarette to the ground and stomps it

out then takes a few steps toward me. She holds her arms out, and I run into them, not even worried about the smoke smell.

She said similar things to me last year. But I'm going to believe them this time, because my heart can't afford not to.

She holds me close, sniffing as she rubs my back.

"I love you, Mom," I tell her.

"I love you too, baby. Thank you for being my rock. I promise, though, I'm going to start being yours."

I say goodbye to Marge and get back in my car, unsure what to do with my now-free Saturday. The swim season hasn't started yet, so I dial Shane, but it goes to voice-mail. I look at the temperature on my dashboard, and I know where he is.

The lake isn't completely frigid yet.

I drive down Lake Shore Highway a bit, turning down his road, passing all the other insane houses on Rich Man's Cove until I pull into the Hunters'. Unsurprisingly, Dr. Hunter's Mercedes is not in the driveway, but Shane's truck is. I hop out of my car and follow the stone path that leads from the driveway around to the back of the house. I take it all the way down the backyard to the edge of the dock and walk down to the very end. And then I see him, swimming like he normally does this time of year, from his family's dock all the way out to the docks two hundred or so yards away.

I watch as he reaches up to touch the other dock then turns back in my direction. His form is perfect, and as he gets closer, I can make out every line, every ridge of his muscles he puts so much work into. The look on his face is fierce and intense, like the chilly fall air and the undoubtedly freezing water has no effect on him whatsoever. I'm completely enamored, watching him swim. Watching him take such care, exuding so much passion for something.

It makes me want to be the water, his hands diving in, learning how to navigate me.

I want to wrap around every inch of his body, letting him lead me with the tenacity he has as he rides the wakes from the boats that speed by.

But then I see it.

The boat that's way too close to the docks.

The boat that's coming at him.

The driver that doesn't see him.

And my whole world stops. I jump up and down at the edge of the dock, waving my hands and screaming.

The driver is bent over, reaching for something on the boat.

Shane stops in the water, looking at me then turning toward the boat. When he sees that it's coming at him, he starts swimming sideways, desperately trying to get out of its path.

I scream as loud as I can, but it doesn't seem to be doing anything over the roar of the boat's engine. I look around, looking for something to throw, something that can help. I hop onto the Hunters' pontoon, looking around. I see a whistle hanging from the gear shift, and I snatch it, running to the nose of the boat. I stand on the very edge and start blowing until, finally, the driver looks up. I point at Shane in the water, and his eyes grow wide. He yanks on the wheel at the last moment, and at the same time, I see Shane take in a breath and dive down under the surface.

It feels like hours have passed, and when the boat is a few yards off the path of Shane, he kills the engine.

But Shane hasn't come back up.

I yank my jacket off, take a step back, and dive in, swimming in the direction where he went down.

"Shane!" I start to scream, pushing my way through the chilly water. "Shane!" I dive under, trying like hell to open my eyes in the murky lake water, but it's no use. I may as well be in the pitch black. I come back up, turning from side to side.

Then he pops up, flinging his head to the side and gasping for air.

I've never felt so much in my whole life.

I swim to him, throwing my arms around his neck, making us both bob up and down in the water.

"Oh my god!" I scream. Then I pull him away from me, looking at his face, his head, for any sign of any sort of injury. "Did he hit you? Are you okay?"

He shakes his head, treading the water.

"What...what are you doing out here?" he asks.

"I...I was on the dock, and I saw you go down," I say.

"Did you jump in after me?" he asks. I nod. He pulls me in closer and rests his forehead against mine, closing his eyes as we tread the choppy water. "Jules, you could have..." he starts to say, shaking his head.

I know. I thought the same about you.

I reach my arms out again, holding his face in my hands. I start to shake, and I'm not sure if it's from the water or from the state of shock.

"I don't know how you do this. It's f-f-fucking f-f-freezing in here," I tell him. He nods.

"Let's get out," he says. As we get back to the dock,

he pulls himself up onto the wood then reaches down for my hands, pulling me out of the water like I'm weightless. He's shirtless, but I'm the one shivering when we get out. He grabs his sweat jacket off the dock and wraps it around me.

"You all okay?" we hear the driver call out to us. Shane waves him off, but I feel rage boiling inside of me.

"Try looking the next time, asshole!" I yell out, and Shane whips his head to me. My eyes widen when I realize I've said it out loud, but I don't regret it.

He could have killed Shane, and the thought makes me sick to my stomach.

Shane wraps his arm around me, running his hand up and down on my arm to try and get some warmth back into me as we make our way back onto land.

"He almost hit you," I whisper when we reach the grass. Saying the words out loud, the thought of it makes me feel nauseous. It makes me feel weak, my legs like cement. The thought of life without him makes me feel so unsettled that I start to shake. This past summer up here, there was an accident. A couple of kids from school were racing boats at night and crashed into the dam.

One of those kids was Ryder.

The other was a kid from out of town, who also happened to be the brother of Ryder's girlfriend.

Her family took off and hasn't come back. There's supposed to be a trial in a few months for Ryder. But whenever we see him, it's like the life is gone from him already. Like being found innocent wouldn't change his will for life.

That's how I would feel, I think, if anything had happened to Shane today.

I don't know what's more terrifying: the thought of him not being around, or the realization that I don't know what my life would look like if he wasn't in it.

My mother's words ring in my ear.

The truth is, sweetie, I don't really know who I am without him.

I shake my head.

You're not the same as her. And Shane is most definitely not the same as Dad.

But as we walk up the grass, my legs get heavier and heavier, the shock of what just happened finally hitting me, and I lock up, freezing in place. He turns to me, eyes narrowing on my face.

"Hey, Jules," he whispers, wrapping his arms around me and pulling me into his chest. "I'm okay."

His bare chest is cold against my face, but feeling his skin on mine is exactly what I need to ground me and bring me back down to earth.

He's still here. He's okay.

After a few moments of standing there like that, he pulls me apart from him, holding me at arm's length. He reaches his thumb up to swipe away a single tear that's rolling down my cheek, and then he smiles.

"I can't believe you jumped in after me," he whispers. I swallow and shrug.

"You might be fast, but I didn't think you were fast enough to outswim a speedboat," I say. He laughs and pulls me in again.

"Grey, you're the best damn friend I ever had," he says as we finish the walk up to the house. I draw in a long breath as he opens the back door, that half-smile killing me.

Hunter, you're everything.

14

"I really can't believe all it took was some hot chocolate and a smile from old blue eyes to get you to see him again," Kirby calls to me from my bed. She's in between shifts and stopped by to raid my kitchen and give me more shit for agreeing to go to Shane's party today. I'm in my bathroom, combing through my thick copper mane and deciding, after too much deliberating, that it's just going to stay down like it almost always does.

I walk out and huff at her, grabbing the shirt I laid out on my chair and tugging it on.

"You need a better bra," she says, looking me up and down as she pops another bite of last night's pasta into her mouth.

"This bra is fine," I tell her. "We weren't all born as well-endowed as you, my dear cousin."

She rolls her eyes then looks down at her chest.

"They really are a gift from God, aren't they?" she says. I laugh and roll my eyes, taking one more look in the mirror. She looks at me again, tilting her head to one side. "You really think you can do this?"

I turn to face her.

"Do what? Go to a birthday party? Yeah, I think I can handle that." I laugh nervously.

"You know that's not what I mean," she says, and I feel the tone of the whole room growing more serious. She puts her fork down and leans in my direction. "I know that losing Tommy like that changed you. But when Shane left, that *broke* you, ya know? I'm not blaming you for it, and I'm not calling you weak. I'm just saying that you have had to do a lot of work over the last decade to get yourself where you wanted to be. Without him."

I grab the side of my arm, looking out the window.

"If you want him back in your life, then I want that for you, Jules. I just want to make sure it's *this* Jules that's deciding. Not the one standing on the shore before she stepped out onto that ice eleven years ago."

"Thank you, Kirb," I tell her, leaning forward to pat her shoulder. "I appreciate you always looking out for me. Really. But he just wants to be friends again. No harm in that, right?"

She gives me a reluctant nod, and I'm pretty sure the inner Jules is face-palming *so* hard right now. But I ignore them both and grab my purse off my dresser.

"Did you get him a gift?" she asks. I draw in a long breath and nod, walking out to the living room and grabbing the bag then bringing it back in and handing it to her. She looks up at me suspiciously. She takes the bag and reaches inside, pulling out the frame I had packed in there.

She studies the faded photo for a minute then looks up at me.

"This is...this is perfect," she says, tucking it back in the bag.

"I found it when I first moved in," I say. "Feels like it's too good of a shot to be in a box." She nods.

"Definitely too good," she says. I pull my coat on and take the bag.

"Don't forget to lock up when you leave," I call to her.

"Have fun," she calls back.

When I pull into the Hunters' driveway, the most intense deja vu I've ever experienced hits me before I even put the car in park. How many times we pulled into this house. How many nights I spent here. I grab the gift and my purse and head up to the front porch. I raise my hand to knock, but before my knuckles touch the wood, the door swings open.

"There she is!" Mrs. Hunter shrieks, pulling me in for a hug like I didn't just see her earlier in the week.

"Hey, Mrs. Hunter," I say, patting her back. "I'm just gonna set this down, and I'll grab the cupcakes from the car."

"Oh, let me get Shane to help," she says.

"Oh, no, I'm fi—"

"Shane! Jules is here. Come help with the cupcakes," she calls into the house before I can say anything.

I turn and walk back to my car, opening the trunk and leaning in to grab the two cupcake containers I scooped up from the bakery on my way.

"Hey," he says, leaning in next to me to grab one

from my hand. "Thank you for these. And thank you for coming."

"Hey," I say, breathless. "Of course."

He looks through the frosted lid, trying to see what I've devised for him.

"What theme did you go with?" he asks. I shrug playfully.

"Guess you'll just have to wait till cake time to see," I say. He smiles and nods. We walk up the front steps, but just as we reach the door, he pauses and grabs my arm.

"Thanks for coming, Jules. Feels like old times," he says with a soft smile. I can't help but reciprocate it; there's something about a happy Shane that makes me all giddy.

"Thanks for inviting me," I say. "Or maybe I should thank your mom?" He grins again and gives me a look then opens the door for me.

I walk straight into the house and into the kitchen, setting the cupcakes down on the center of the huge oak table that Mrs. Hunter had custom-made years ago. I put my gift on the smaller table in the living room then head back into the kitchen to set the cupcakes up. I'm grateful to have something to do so that I don't have to jump right back into my past; I need a little bit of a buffer.

"There she is," I hear Dr. Hunter's hearty voice say from behind me. I spin around and wrap him in a big hug.

"Dr. Hunter!" I say, genuinely happy to see him. I always had a fondness for Dr. Hunter. I always found it so endearing, the way that he took in the boys and truly made them into who they became. Some of Shane's best qualities came straight from Dr. Hunter, whether or not his blood ran through Shane's veins. They were a family, in every sense of the word.

"How have you been, dear?" he asks before setting me down.

"Oh, I've been great," I say. "How have you been? I was telling Mrs. Hunter that I will have to stop by and visit more often."

"We would love that," he says. "Just because our boys ran off doesn't mean you have to."

He says it with a sad smile, and I think we share the same sentiments.

"Oh. My. Gosh," Mrs. Hunter cries in her sing-song voice as she makes her way back into the kitchen from greeting the other guests. "Those are *perfect!*"

I'm almost done setting the cupcakes up, tiers of cupcakes covered in green icing leading up to the extra-large cupcake on top, topped in blue icing with a swimmer figurine on top. I added pine trees to the tops of some of the others, and white clouds that stick out from the top tier.

Along the sides of the hill, I added other little hints of Shane: a bag of Hot Fries, an energy drink, a boat.

And at the very bottom, I added two tiny figurines, one with short brown hair, and the other with long, copper-colored locks. I know not everyone else will get the meaning behind it all. But I know he will.

"The Dream Team," I hear Shane whisper from behind me, and it makes me jump. He steps up so that his chest is almost touching my back, and the breath runs from my lungs.

"Yep," I whisper back.

"I love it, Jules," he whispers before stepping around

me and scoping out the rest of the cupcakes. He looks up at me and smiles.

"Hot Fries and energy drinks," he says. I shrug.

"Guess you weren't the only one who didn't forget," I tell him.

"Hot damn, she's a pro!" Derrick says as he walks into the kitchen, admiring my work. He kisses my cheek then pulls Shane in for a hug, Kaylee shuffling behind him with a bowl of pasta salad.

The rest of the crowd makes their way in, some flowing out onto the Hunters' extravagant deck and patio that we spent so many nights on as kids, some staying inside to escape the impending cold.

I wrap my scarf around my neck and walk out the back door to where my friends sit, huddled around the firepit. I swear, from the looks of it, I've stepped back in time.

"Well, isn't this just a blast from the past," I say as I walk up behind them, putting my hands on the back of Luna's and Ryder's chairs.

"We were just talking about the time that you and Tommy did that dance on the edge of the dock when Shane won states," Derrick says. "And you did that jump and busted your ass."

Everyone bursts into laughter, including me.

"Well, not everyone can be as graceful as me, what can I say." I laugh, grabbing the chair next to Luna and sitting down.

"You guys were the best damn cheerleaders," Shane says, his eyes on mine. "I always knew no matter how bad I might have sucked, the two of you would act like I was a damn king."

"Except that you never sucked," Ryder says, and the rest of the group agrees.

"Oh my gosh, remember how pissed off Tanya and the other girls used to get when Jules and you would—" Luna starts to say between laughter, but her voice slows as she realizes what she's bringing up. My eyes narrow on her, and she swallows.

"They knew Jules was my best girl," Shane says with a deadly half-smile as he leans back in his chair. "And my best pool partner." I can feel eyes bouncing back and forth between us, and butterflies swirl in my stomach. *That night on the pool table…*

I have to change directions here.

"And Tommy was our best guy." I smile back. He nods slowly, and the group grows quiet.

"To Tommy," Ryder says, holding his beer up.

"To Tommy," we all echo, beers in the air. Mrs. Hunter calls down over the deck railing, telling everyone to come in for cupcakes. We all sing, Shane looking simultaneously completely embarrassed but also so happy.

My heart swells in my chest.

After cupcakes, I stay inside to help Mrs. Hunter clean up some, despite her efforts at shooing me back out with the rest of my friends.

"Honey, you should get back out there," she tells me again.

"I will, I promise," I say. "Just want to get these covered up." I pull what's left of the cupcakes and put them on a platter, trying to keep them as intact as possible.

"Those were a hit," she tells me as she dries another pot. I nod.

"I'm glad," I tell her.

"I'm sure it was a bit jarring for you to see him again after all this time," she says, making my spine go straight. I turn to her as she looks out the giant windows that overlook the backyard, gazing down lovingly at her son.

"It was, uh...a bit of a shock, I guess." I chuckle nervously, trying to find something else to clean or put away.

"He was in such a dark place after Tommy died," she says, turning the sink off and drying her hands. She turns to me and leans back against the counter. "When he told us he wanted to graduate early, we knew it was bad," she says.

I put the last of the plates in the trash and turn to her, leaning back against the table. I nod.

"I understand," I tell her. She nods.

"I know you do, honey," she says. "Better than anyone. I think that's why he just sort of...took off, ya know?"

My eyes find hers, searching for more.

"I think he thought he was doing right by you," she tells me, and I don't know how to respond.

Doing right by me? By leaving me without a word?

But that's a conversation I should have with him, not with his mother. She turns to the window again.

"It's good having him home. I'll miss him when he leaves again," she says.

"Do you know, uh, how long that'll be?" I ask. She shakes her head.

"I guess it depends on these deals he's trying to make. If he gets the promotion, I'm afraid he'll return to

California and *never* come back," she says with a sad smile. I nod and force a grin.

"As long as he's happy," I say. She nods and pats my hand.

By the time we're done cleaning up, most of the guests have started to leave, and Shane makes his way into the kitchen.

"What are you two up to?" he asks, snagging a carrot from the veggie tray.

"Just cleaning up," Mrs. Hunter says. "What a fun night. Did you have fun, honey?"

He leans over and kisses her cheek.

"Yes, Mom," he says. "Best birthday party ever." She takes his face in her hands and kisses both his cheeks.

"It's so good to have you home," she says before patting his arm and walking out into the living room. "Your father and I are going to go meet a few friends at Lou's. We'll be back soon." He nods as she walks by.

There's an awkward silence, and it scares me, because the things that aren't being said are the things that are loudest. And they're the things that might kill me.

So I fill it.

"So," I say, crossing my arms over my chest. "The pool table reference, huh?"

He laughs and drops his head then lifts his eyes back up to me slowly.

"Wasn't sure if you'd catch that," he says. I smile and shake my head.

"Not much gets by me," I say. He motions to the cupcakes with his head.

"Thanks again for those," he says. "They were

perfect. If I were a batch of cupcakes, I would be those ones."

I laugh.

"I wasn't sure if it all still represented you," I say, "but I had to go from memory."

"It all still represents me," he says.

"Do you still swim?"

He nods.

"Yep. Try to get in the water a few times a week. What about you? You still bad at it?" he asks.

I burst with laughter.

"Why yes," I say with a nod. "Yes, I am."

He smiles, and his eyes trail across the room to the window then back to me.

"Care to test your skills?" he asks, a mischievous look in his eyes. "See if you've gotten any better?"

I follow his gaze to the window then back to him, and I raise an eyebrow.

"No way," I say with a shake of my head. "It's freezing. And I don't have a change of clothes."

He shrugs, backing toward the glass doors.

"That never stopped the Jules I knew," he says.

The Jules you knew never came out of that lake.

But never one to back down from a challenge, I roll my eyes and surrender, following him out the back door. Goosebumps pop up all over my skin the second the wind blows, and I know how brutal the water is going to be.

But he's already kicking off his shoes.

"Let's do this, Grey," he says. I shake my head again, but he smiles. We both know I'm going in that water.

He turns and starts jogging toward the dock, and I

let out the breath I've been holding so I can catch up with him.

When we get to the edge, we stop, looking out over the water. He turns and looks down at me then wraps his arms around my waist and jumps.

I'm pretty sure the blood freezes in my veins the second we go under. I've never been this fucking cold in my whole life.

That's a lie.

But when I feel his hand wrap around my waist, pulling us up to the surface, I feel a little bit warmer. I flip my hair back over my head and open my eyes, the freezing water making my limbs feel as heavy as lead.

"Jesus, this still sucks," I mutter as I wipe the water away from my face. He laughs as he swims closer so that our faces are just inches apart.

"You haven't changed a bit, Jules." He chuckles, his thick locks curling and falling into a perfect tousled mess on his head. His eyes are piercing in the last of the sunlight, and I blink and look away before they see too much.

"I've changed," I tell him, my tone more serious. He paddles in closer.

"I thought I did, too," he says, and then I can feel his finger curling around my arm. "Till I came back here."

My heart is skipping beats in my chest, not sure whether to slow from the cold or speed up from his skin on mine. I catch my breath and tug my arm from his grasp. I turn and swim to the dock, pulling myself up onto the wood. I squeeze the excess water from my hair and throw it over one shoulder then start to walk off the dock. I hear him get out, the patter of his feet against the wood as he follows behind.

"Jules," he says. I stop at the end of the dock and turn toward him.

This feels like it's getting heavy.

It has to stay light.

"I'm just cold," I tell him, although I know it's pointless for me to lie. His eyes drop to the ground.

"Well, let me at least give you a change of clothes," he says. I think for a moment then nod. I will freeze where I stand if I keep these clothes on any longer.

I follow him into the house and up the large wooden staircase, and before I know it, I'm standing in Shane Hunter's bedroom. This can't be a good idea.

15

FALL OF SENIOR YEAR

"I need more tokens, please," I call over the counter, jiggling my empty cup. Shane looks at me and shakes his head before walking to the drawer.

"How many is that now, a thousand?" he asks. I smile as he dumps another handful of them into my cup.

"Give or take," I say with an innocent shrug.

"Hey, don't stop her," Tommy says from behind me, broom and dustpan in hand. "She's gonna win the jackpot at that Ring of Light game, and we'll all be able to retire. Don't stand in the way of greatness." Shane rolls his eyes.

"That's right," I say with a playful nod in his direction. "Don't stop greatness."

The corner of Shane's lips pulls up, flashing me those perfect teeth.

"Never," he says. I feel fire in my cheeks as I turn back to Luna and Kirby, carefully shaking my ass a little as I do, hoping my best friend might still be watching.

"Did ya get more?" Luna asks, waiting with her hands out like a child.

"You know I did," I tell her, dumping some of my stash into her palms.

"Of course she did. She's got the employees of the month drooling over her," Kirby says, shifting in her seat as she sips on her blue Icee while Luna plays the claw game for the hundredth time since we've been here.

We might be a little too old for some of these arcade games, but when the summer season dies down and it's too early for snow, it's one of the only things to do around here. Plus, the special treatment from having my two best friends work here doesn't suck, either.

"Oh, stop it," I say, swatting Kirby away as I stand next to Luna to watch her catch—and drop—another stuffed animal. "They do not."

"Ha," Kirby says, rolling her eyes. "Luna, back me up here."

"Damnit!" Luna shouts as the claw drags back across to its rightful place, empty yet again. She blows a strand of her jet-black hair out of her face and turns to me.

"They kinda drool over you, Jules," she says. I raise my eyebrows, totally expecting Luna to have my back. I look over to the counter where they're taking cards and handing out tokens, totally in sync, like they own the place.

"That's bull," I say. "They're just my friends."

"Whatevs," Kirby says. "I'm just callin' it like I see it. Especially Shane." My head whips to hers.

"What about Shane?" I ask.

"He looks at you more than you look at him," she says, and Luna snorts. I playfully shove her and shoot

Kirby daggers with my eyes. "Don't shoot the messenger. I'm just saying, it's bound to happen."

I shake my head.

No. It can't happen.

"That's not true," I say, my eyes trailing across the arcade to Shane again. "We're not...we're not right for each other that way. Friends. That's it."

"Wouldn't it be easier to just bang and get it over with?" Kirby asks, sucking the cup dry. Luna bursts out laughing.

"What's so funny over here?" we hear Tommy ask as he comes around the corner, his black uniform polo wrinkled and tucked in on only one side. He throws his arm around Luna's shoulder, who gently shimmies from underneath him as if Daniel has eyes somewhere in here.

Honestly, knowing him, he just might.

"Oh, we were just telling my dear cousin here how you and Sh—"

"A*hem,*" I say in her direction, my eyes wide. "I was just asking *my* dear cousin if she wanted to die a slow and painful death."

Tommy's eyes bounce from Kirby to me, but before he can ask anything more, a loud raucous erupts from the front of the room. My eyes land on Shane, who has come out from behind the counter. The look in his eyes is one I've seen just one other time—at the first party I went to.

Anger.

No, not just anger.

Pure rage.

Tommy leaps across the floor toward him, and I'm not far behind.

"What the *fuck* are you doing here?" Shane asks, and Tommy and I turn to see a man standing across from him, built a lot like Shane. Similar grayish-blue eyes, same stature with a little extra gut.

And then Tommy and I look at each other because we come to the realization at the same time.

It's his father.

"What's goin' on here, Shane?" Tommy asks, walking slowly toward him, his hands raised, positioning himself between Shane and his father. But Shane doesn't answer. He clenches his hands into fists, his shoulders moving up and down with every labored breath he takes. By now, the entire arcade has stopped whatever game they're playing and is turned toward us.

"I came to see my son," the man says, and I see Shane grit his teeth, his jaw clenching.

"You need to leave," Shane growls, and I swear I can hear my own heartbeat. The manager, Bobby, emerges from the back to see what's going on. Tommy holds his hands up.

"I got it, Bobby," he says. "I got it."

"Get them out of here," Bobby says.

"Come on, Shane, let's step outside," Tommy whispers then turns to Mr. Doyle. "Sir, we need you to step out of the building."

Mr. Doyle's eyes narrow on Shane, but he backs out of the doors and into the lot.

Once it's clear there's nothing to see, the rest of the arcade goes back to whatever game they were more than likely losing. But I keep my eyes on Shane. Tommy has his hand pressed to Shane's chest, and I know it's both to calm him and to keep him where he stands.

"Let's let him leave, buddy, okay? Let's let him

leave," he says calmly. But I see the moment Shane breaks. The moment he loses control.

"Shane!" I call out, but he can't hear me. He bursts through the glass doors into the parking lot, Tommy and I right on his tail.

"Shane!" Tommy yells, but he doesn't stop.

When we get outside, Mr. Doyle is standing, backed up against a giant red pickup truck. When he sees us, he chuckles.

"I knew you couldn't just let it go," he says. "You do have my blood after all."

Tommy positions himself between the two of them again.

"Shane, let's go back inside," he whispers. "He's not worth it." Shane's eyes narrow on his father, and I think I can feel every ounce of pain that's oozing out of him right now.

"What are you doing here?" he asks.

"Word is, you're pretty good at swimming," Mr. Doyle says, and all of our eyes find him. He's not bad-looking—or at least, he wouldn't be if he actually took care of himself. His face is unshaven, his hair sticking out from his backwards trucker hat. His boots are covered in dried mud, and his jeans are tattered at the bottom.

But his eyes. His eyes are what get me. They look so much like Shane's. *He* looks so much like Shane. But that anger that Shane only exhibits once in a blue moon…that anger is plastered on his father's face like it consumes him. Like it eats him alive.

"Did you know I was a swimmer back in the day?" he asks. Shane lets out a breath.

"Of course I didn't know that," he says. "I don't know a damn thing about you."

"Yeah?" Mr. Doyle says, pushing off his car. "And whose fuckin' fault is that?"

Flames seem to erupt behind Shane's eyes, and he takes a step in the direction of his father. Tommy squares up so that he's completely in front of Shane now, and Mr. Doyle laughs.

"You wanna step to me, son?" he asks. "Ask your little boyfriend to step aside. We can settle this like grown men." Tommy turns slightly but stops himself from looking at Mr. Doyle.

"*Why* are you *here?*" Shane growls again, his knuckles white.

"I came to check in on you," Mr. Doyle says, holding his hands out. "Heard my boy was takin' after his old man. Thought I'd come see what that was all about."

"I'm not your boy," Shane says under his breath. "And I don't take after you one bit. You don't get to come back in here after all these years, after all this time, after my *mother* put all this work into Ty and me, and get any of the goddamn credit."

My heart is breaking, because through his intense glare, through his hate-fueled words, I can hear the crack of his heart breaking, the cry of a little boy whose father broke his heart.

"Hey, now, calm down, son," Mr. Doyle says, his lips turning into a snake-like smile. "Diane left *me*, remember?"

"Because you couldn't keep your fucking hands off of her!" Shane says, and I take a step toward him. He's seething now, and I can feel the heat radiating off of him.

Tommy's still standing hard and fast between them, and I step in front of him, placing my hand on his chest. Finally, he breaks his glare, his eyes dropping down to me.

"It's okay," I tell him, willing him to feel my calm, to feel my peace. "Let's go back inside. You don't owe him any of your time."

I say it all loud enough for Mr. Doyle to hear. I want him to know how much he's missed out on. How big of a mistake he made. How wonderful his son became in *spite* of him.

I can feel his heart rate slow beneath my hand. He puts his hand on mine and nods, turning slowly toward the doors.

"Boy, you can avoid me all you want to. But it's still my blood that runs through your body. It's *me* that's a part of you. Not that soft-ass doctor. You remember that." Mr. Doyle turns on his heel and pulls the door of his truck open. "You can't fight biology, son. And we all turn into our fathers eventually."

I feel a shift in the wind; I feel the change in my Shane. Before Tommy or I can stop him, he turns back to his father, flying across the parking lot. He has him by the collar of his shirt, slamming him up against his truck. He cocks his arm back and lands one punch to his father's jaw just as Tommy and I reach him. Tommy grabs his arms, putting him into a hold as Mr. Doyle falls to the ground. Shane wriggles in his grasp, trying like hell to get back to his father. I stand in front of him, grabbing his face in my hands.

"Shane! Shane, look at me," I say. "Look at me."

And finally, he does.

"You are Shane Hunter."

His eyes bore into mine, like he's begging me to go on.

"Shane *Hunter*. And you are the best damn friend we have ever had. You know who you are. He doesn't."

I see his body go limp, and Tommy loosens his grip. I take Shane's hands and pull him away from the truck. Tommy pulls Mr. Doyle to his feet and opens his truck door again.

"Mr. Doyle, kindly get in your truck, drive away, and never fucking come back," he orders. "There's no use for you here." Mr. Doyle hocks up a bloody loogie at Shane's feet, and with one final glare, slams his truck door and speeds away.

As he does, Tommy walks toward us, putting a hand on Shane's shoulder.

"You good, man?" he asks. Shane nods slowly.

"Yeah," he says. "Sorry."

Tommy shakes his head, giving Shane a soft nudge to the jaw.

"Anything for you, boo," he says, and Shane can't help but smile. "I'm gonna go let Bobby know we're all good."

I turn to Shane, but his eyes are on the ground, filled with shame.

"Hey," I say. Slowly, he lifts those eyes to me.

"He only came back because I'm worth something now," he whispers. My heart splinters in my chest, and I wrap my arms around him. I feel his shoulders shudder, and I realize that seeing Shane hurt is one of the greatest fears of my life.

I wrap my arms around his shoulders tighter and pull him into me. He buries his face in my hair, and I run my hand up and down the back of his neck.

"Shane, you've *always* been worth something," I tell him, holding him out away from me so that I can look into his eyes. "Always. You're kind, and giving, and talented, and with you, I always feel…" I pause for a moment, feeling my own emotions taking over. I let out a long breath. "With you, I always feel safe."

His eyes widen as he stares down at me.

"*You* are my safe place, Shane. You are *not* him."

I see tears at the brims of his eyes, and he wraps his arms around me again, pulling me back into him.

And as we stand here, holding each other in this parking lot, I feel a moment of panic.

Shane is my safe place. I can't lose him. Which means I have to learn how to not love him.

16

"This should work just for the ride home," he says, handing me a t-shirt from the dresser. He sniffs it before he hands it over, and I raise an eyebrow. "Mom kept all my stuff that I didn't take. I just wanted to make sure it's not musty."

I smile and take the shirt, pressing it to my face.

"It's not musty," I say. "It still smells like you." Our eyes meet, and he clears his throat.

"You can, uh, change in the bathroom."

I nod and walk by him, careful to leave plenty of space between us. I strip down out of my soaked jeans and shirt and tug the shirt on over my head. I let out a quiet laugh when I look at myself in the mirror: long, copper locks, cold and wet, hanging over a faded Meade High Swimming t-shirt. One I'm pretty sure I've worn before. I pull on the old sweatpants he gave me along with it and roll them at the waist a few times.

When I open the door, my jaw drops when I see him, shirtless, digging through his suitcase that's splayed out on his bed. He lifts his eyes to me, peering at me through a single dark curl that's fallen over his eye.

I melt where I stand, a full-blown puddle.

My ex-best friend is fucking gorgeous.

He was beautiful then. But *now*…my, has he grown. His chest is broader, the muscles across it flexing with every move he makes. I follow the curves of it down to the peaks and valleys of his abs, which are somehow even more defined than when he was a state champ swimmer.

But as I come to and catch myself staring, I realize he's doing the same.

He stands slowly, and I suddenly become very aware that his eyes are scouring me from head to toe.

"Wow," he says barely above a whisper. I bite my bottom lip.

"What?"

He shakes his head.

"Nothin'," he says. "You just…you still look good in my clothes."

I swallow and tuck a piece of hair behind my ear.

"Well, uh, thanks for these. I guess I should be—"

"You wanna go for a ride?" he asks. I cock my head to the side.

"A ride? To where?"

He shrugs, giving me that devilish smile.

"Wherever we want." I let out a long sigh.

"Fine," I say with a smile I'm trying to stifle. "Let's do it, Hunter."

He tugs a shirt over his head, and I take a mental picture of him before it covers him completely. He grabs a sweatshirt then digs into his bag and pulls out another one, tossing it to me. I stare down at it, my mouth running dry.

I want you to steal my hoodies, too.

I swallow again and tug it on over my head, basking in the scent of him, imagining him wrapping himself around me.

WE GET into his rental and start driving, and the first stop we make is to get hot cocoa and trail mix. He won't let me pay for anything, and although it's a sweet gesture, I don't like it. I don't want him to feel like I can't handle myself, my own expenses. He's missed a lot over the last decade or so, and one of those things is that I got my financial shit together. I don't take after my mom.

"So," I say, tugging open the bag of trail mix and shoveling some out. "Where to?"

"Wherever you want," he says. I laugh as I start to dig through, plucking out all the raisins. When I have a solid stash, I hold them out in front of him, and he opens his palm. He looks down at them and smiles before popping them into his mouth.

"Still weird, I see," I say with a smile, shaking my head.

"Look who's talking. You still only eat the peanuts?" he asks. I smile and nod.

"Bet your ass."

"Weirdo," he says with a playful nudge. We drive a little bit farther down the road, and then he stops when we come to the fork. To the left, we'll travel farther into town. To the right, we'll head into the state park—the one where me, and him, and Tommy always went. Our secret, secluded spot.

The spot where everything changed.

I see his Adam's apple bob while he silently deliberates. I slide my hand onto his, and he looks at me.

"It's okay," I whisper. "We don't have to."

His eyes are big, like wide saucers, and he blinks once or twice before veering to the right. I swallow, settling deeper into my seat. I've been back to this spot countless times since everything happened, replaying the good times, fending off the bad, drowning in every experience I ever had here. But I take it from the look on Shane's face that he hasn't set foot back here since the night Tommy died.

He parks the car and gets out, letting out a breath through pursed lips. We look at each other again then head down the overgrown trail we used to take so often. When we get to the clearing, I suck in a long breath, as if I'm taking a drag from a cigarette. It's a beautiful night, the air chilly, the sky a deep navy, making the perfect backdrop for the diamonds that cover it.

I walk down to the edge of the water, staring out over the lake. It'll be frozen soon, covered in snow from storm after storm.

"How can you stand it?" he asks, so close to me it makes me jump.

"Stand what?"

"Being here."

I shrug.

"I can't stand being away."

"Why?" he asks. I turn to face him.

"Because it's home. It may be the site of the worst

day of my life, but it's also the site of all the best ones. It's here where I feel closest to him." I let my eyes drop to the ground. "And after you left, it's where I felt closest to you."

He takes a step closer to me so that I can feel the heat from his body, and he reaches his finger down to lift my chin.

"Jules," he whispers.

I close my eyes. I've worked so hard all these years to move on, move past my life with Shane. Move past the night that everything almost happened, move past the moment where I realized it never would.

And now, standing here at this shore with him, it feels like I've been dropped back to my senior year. Right back to the night it all happened. To that gaping wound that Tommy left and the one that Shane poured salt in.

And I know that if I open my eyes, he'll see it all. He'll see every tear I cried for him; he'll see every memory I've held onto desperately. He'll see every hope I ever had about the two of us sinking beneath a frozen surface.

"Jules, look at me," he whispers. And finally, I drum up the nerve to.

He's your friend. Let him be that.

When I open my eyes, I see his narrowed on me, searching my face. His thumb strokes the side of my cheek, and I swallow.

"I missed you so much when I left," he says, bowing his head. "You have no idea."

I feel a fire burning beneath my chest. Because of *course* I have an idea. Except, *I* am not the one who left. He is. I take a step back out of his reach.

"Can you take me home?" I ask. His eyes narrow again in confusion.

"Jules, can we—"

"I don't want to do this," I say firmly. I turn on my heel and walk toward the path.

"Jules, we should talk about—"

I whip back around to him, my hair cascading all around me.

"You're eleven years too late, Shane," I tell him. "You went and made the life for yourself that we were supposed to make together. But it turns out that staying here in Meade Lake was the best decision I could have ever made. I know who I am. I know who I am without *you*. You didn't exactly give me a choice there. So please, just take me home."

"Jules, that's not... I never meant for that. I didn't want to hurt you or...or leave you."

I take a few steps toward him, and to my surprise, he takes one back, like he's afraid.

"Then why?"

There's a long pause, and I can't hear anything but the wind blowing through what's left of the leaves.

Finally, he drops his eyes to the ground and shakes his head.

"I...I can't."

I feel my heart beating at a rapid pace, as if it's letting me know it's still there, despite his best efforts at crushing it completely.

"Then *please*," I manage to muster, "just take me home."

I turn back around and walk through the trail, waiting by the passenger door for him to unlock it.

A few silent minutes later, he pulls into my driveway.

I open the door and get out, standing silently next to the car. And just before I turn to walk inside, I reach down and pull his hoodie up over my head, tossing it onto the passenger seat of his car.

17

WINTER OF SENIOR YEAR

"Open it!" Shane growls at me as he pops a chip into his mouth. We've been sitting on the shore of the lake on our bench for what feels like an hour now. This winter has been unseasonably warm, and even though we're smack-dab in the middle of what should be the coldest part of the year, Shane and I aren't even wearing gloves. The last few days have felt more like the beginning of spring rather than the dead of winter. I have the letter from USC in my shaking hand, the corner of it creased from me nervously folding it back and forth so many times.

He's been waiting to commit to USC until after I got in, which his parents and everyone else think is idiotic—I have to admit, if it weren't for me, I would think the same—but he doesn't seem to care. It's not like any of the schools that have given him scholarship offers have been bad options, so he's in good shape either way. I turn to him.

"What if…"

He shakes his head, putting his hand on mine to stop it from trembling.

"Don't. You are a straight-A, honor-roll, dream student. There's no way you didn't get in," he says. I swallow. He's probably right. But there's another problem.

"But what if I can't afford it?"

His eyes widen a bit, bouncing back and forth across the frozen lake in front of us. Shane is a do-er, a problem solver, a fixer. Money hasn't really been a problem for Shane. If these scholarships hadn't poured in for him, Dr. and Mrs. Hunter would have had no issue covering his tuition.

"Can you get loans?" he asks. I nod.

"Yeah, I'll have to. But I'm not sure it'll be enough. There would still be room and board and all that. And I—"

"We will figure that out," he says, so sure that it makes me jump back. He lifts his eyes to mine. "Jules, we will...we will figure that all out."

I swallow and nod.

"Okay. But listen, if this doesn't happen for me, you have to—"

"Stop, Jules. Stop. This is gonna happen. For *us.*" He brings his other hand to mine, and I realize his are shaking now. His eyes stare down at our hands piled on top of each other, and then he looks up at me again. "I want this with you, Jules," he says, his voice shaking.

I want to ask him what he means. Does he mean college? Does he mean this next phase of life? Or does he mean...more?

Oh God.

I want more.

I want it with him.

I want *him.*

He's the one who knows the crash and burn that is my relationship with my mom. He knows every peak and valley and asks no questions when we go crashing, full-speed, to the ground.

I'm the one who knows what his father means—and doesn't mean—to him and how badly he wants to outrun biology.

I'm also the one who knows how gentle he is, how kind his hands are, how he could never hurt anyone. How his instincts kick in when I need him.

I want this with him.

Three thousand miles from anyone else that we know.

Three thousand miles from our history as "just friends," fighting off the rumors and dodging glances.

I look up at him, his eyes still pouring into mine, saying everything he hasn't yet.

He wants it, too.

"Hey, hey! Did I miss it?" Tommy calls from around the bend, making his way through the clearing. He's carrying a case of beer in one hand and a pizza in the other, jogging toward us.

Shane and I instinctively scoot a few inches apart, our hands dropping from one another. Our eyes meet one last time before Tommy scoots onto the bench with us, and I think we both know this conversation is just getting started.

"Nope," I say, holding the sealed envelope up.

"She's being a big baby," Shane says with that half-smile.

"Aw, come on, Jules. You know you're a shoe-in," he

says, popping the top off one of the beers and leaning back. "Here. Let me."

I reluctantly hand the envelope over to him, putting my hands on my cheeks and staring down at the ground as he sticks his finger in through the side and begins to tear.

He clears his throat dramatically and stands up, positioning himself in front of us as if we are his audience. Shane reaches out his hand and puts it on my knee. We watch as Tommy reads the first few lines, and then his eyes widen and light up, and Shane and I both know what that means.

"Dear Miss Grey, Congratulations!" Tommy reads. "It is with great pleasure that we inform you you have been accepted into the University of Southern California."

He goes on, but I can't hear the rest. My eyes well with tears as Shane scoops me off the bench, swirling me around. Tommy runs up and joins, both of them hoisting me into a rather uncomfortable group hug, but one that I wouldn't trade for the world.

"Fuck yes!" Tommy shouts, throwing his fist into the air. But as the moment fades, the three of us grow quiet. Because after this moment, the three of us, as we know it, is over. Two of us will leave, and things will never be the same. And I think we are all realizing it at one moment.

Shane's eyes drop to the ground, and Tommy clears his throat again.

"I'm so excited for you guys," Tommy says just above a whisper. "I fucking mean that. You're gonna go and do amazing things. And then you'll both get jobs and be rich and can take care of me."

We laugh, but I can see the hurt and fear behind his eyes. I walk toward him and throw my arms around his neck.

"We're still here, Tom," I tell him. He nods as he wraps his arms around me.

"I know," he says. He squeezes me again before setting me down. Then I recognize that mischievous look in his eye.

"I think it's time to celebrate with some ice dancing," he says, hoisting me up and over his shoulder. He turns and makes a mad dash toward the lake.

"Hey, Tom, wait," Shane calls from behind. "It's like fifty fucking degrees, Tommy."

Through my belly laughs, I hear what he's saying. Shane, always my protector. I see him from over Tommy's shoulder, standing on the edge of the water, his face twisted with worry.

"Get out here, ya big pussy!" Tommy calls. "We're celebratin'!"

He swings me around, laughing as we go. Then he stops, swinging me back around so that he's cradling me in his arms.

"You're amazing, Jules," he says. Then he looks at Shane on shore. "And that guy…he thinks it, too. And I don't know if he's ever gonna tell you. So I'm telling you now. Maybe one of you will—" He stops midway through the sentence.

Then he freezes, looking down at the ice that's cracking around his feet.

"Shit, Jules…" His voice trails off, his eyes moving slowly to the large crack that's shooting across the ice like a bullet.

18

I storm into the house and slam the front door, shivering from the cold. I fill the tea kettle and plop it on the stove then kick my shoes off toward the door.

I haven't been this angry in a long, long time. I swing back against the counter and cross my arms over my chest, letting out a puff of air.

How dare he come back, after all this time, and lure me in again? Just to leave me hanging out there on the ice, like the pathetic teenager he left the first time. No explanations, just empty air, until the space between us spanned three thousand miles.

I walk out the back door onto the deck, staring out over the valley blanketed in a thick layer of white, the moon illuminating the entire town. I clutch the railing, my knuckles turning white, and my body starts to tremble. At first, I think it's from the cold, and then I realize it's from this rage, this panic that's burning within me. This familiar abandonment that I thought I did away with, that I thought I recovered from.

And then I hear a knock on my door.

Normally, I'd suspect Kirby and that she'd lost her key like she's already done twice before. But I haven't called Kirby yet. I've just been sitting, stewing, working my way through the events of the last hour.

When I get back through the house and look out the window, I want to curl into a ball on the floor, hide until he gives up and leaves. But I can't.

I sigh and open the door.

"Yes?" I ask him. He's staring down at a frame in his hands—the one I gave him for his birthday. A framed photo of him and me, perched on the edge of his truck cab. Tommy kneels behind us, his arms draped around both of our shoulders, pulling us in close.

Slowly, he lifts his eyes to mine.

"I was gonna let you go," he says quietly, "and give you a little space. But then I saw this, and I realized we need to finish the conversation."

I swallow and cross my arms over my chest. I tap my foot as I contemplate whether or not to take him up on it, then I succumb and step out onto the porch. I pull the door closed behind me.

"We can talk out here," I tell him, my arms still crossed tightly across my chest. If I let him in my house, it's one step closer to letting him back in altogether. And we cannot have that.

He tilts his head for a moment then nods. He holds up the frame.

"This is...this is perfect," he says, sliding it back into the gift bag and setting it down on the porch. "Thank you."

I nod.

"I found it in some of my things when I moved in," I

tell him. "And I just felt like it deserved a frame and some time in the sun."

He smiles and nods.

"It definitely does."

There's an awkward silence, and I walk toward the railing of the porch and lean back against it. My feet are cold on the bare wood, but I'm thinking this will be a quick conversation. I stare at him, eyes wide, waiting for him to start. I said what I needed to say on that bench. I asked what I needed to ask. It's his turn.

He clears his throat and lifts those eyes to me.

"How much do you remember about that night, Jules?" I think for a moment and wrap my arms tighter around my body.

"Um," I mumble awkwardly. It's been years since I've had to recount that night. I mean, I think about it every single day. But it's been forever since I've really had to go back, retrace my steps, remember all the horrific details, delve into the trauma. I regain a little bit of my composure and look up at him. "I remember Tommy carrying me out there. I remember the ice cracking. And then, uh, I remember being in your truck, I think."

He nods.

"You were. What else?"

"Uh, I guess the next thing I remember is waking up in the hospital. And I remember you telling me... I remember hearing about Tommy."

There's another silence, but this one is filled with the palpable feeling of two people who are enduring some painful flashbacks.

"I remember you... I remember you getting into my

bed with me. And then," I say, looking back at him, "I remember you leaving."

He nods slowly then moves to stand in front of me so that he's leaning against the house.

"I was afraid of that," he says just above a whisper.

"Afraid of what?"

"Afraid you wouldn't remember all of it," he says, running a hand through those delicious locks. I shift uncomfortably on my feet.

"What do you mean?"

He sighs and walks forward to the step and sits down. I open the front door and reach for my boots then join him on the step. It feels like this conversation could be a little longer than I thought.

I lean back against the railing, careful to keep distance between us. He lets out a long breath and turns to me.

"When the ice first cracked, I told Tommy just to hold as still as possible, but since he was holding you, the weight wasn't distributed right. You were only a few yards out, but when I realized it was gonna get worse, I started to look around for a rope or a branch that would be long enough to get to you," he says. I nod slowly. Cloudy, frozen memories start to come a little more into focus. "But when I turned back around, it had given way, and you'd both fallen in. I had gotten a branch and crawled out a tiny bit where I knew it was still shallow and stuck the branch out toward you guys."

I nod.

"I do remember that," I whisper.

"But the cold started to kick in, and Tommy started to panic. He moved closer toward you, and I realized he was going to push you out of the way to get to it."

I suck in a long breath as he looks down at his hands. I look down at them, too, and I realize they're trembling.

"It was cracking more, and I knew you'd both been in too long," he says. "I had to make a choice."

He lifts his eyes to me slowly, and I can feel my heart pounding in my ears.

"And I chose you."

19

WINTER OF SENIOR YEAR

"Guys? Shit, guys!" I hear Shane call from the shore. We're only, maybe, twenty yards from the shoreline, but as the ground beneath us literally crumbles, we might as well be a mile out.

"Oh God," I whisper.

"Tommy, don't move too quickly," Shane calls. "Fuck! I gotta find something!" I see him turning around frantically, looking for something, anything, he can use to help us. "My fucking phone is in my truck!" he calls out.

I close my eyes and swallow, but another deafening crack of the ice below us sends my eyes fluttering back open.

"Tom, can you set her down gently? And then both of you get to your bellies as slowly and carefully as you can," Shane directs.

"Tommy…" I say.

"Jules, I'm sorry, I—"

And then we fall. The ice beneath his feet disappears, and the first thing that registers is pain. Freezing pain, like my blood has turned to ice in my veins. We push up to the surface, and my limbs immediately grow heavy. Everything feels like it weighs a million pounds, pulling me down as I try desperately to keep my head above.

"Guys! Fuck!" I hear Shane call as my jaw starts to tremble.

"Help!" Tommy screams from a few feet away. I feel the splashes from his flailing arms. I see him out of the corner of my eye. "Help!"

"Jules! Listen to me!" Shane calls, and I look up to see him on his belly, slowly and steadily crawling out toward me.

"Sh-Shane, don't," I try to muster, but it's no use.

"Jules, listen! As soon as this gets to you, I need you to grab it, okay?" he calls. I see the edge of a long sapling that he's pulled from the ground. But just as it reaches me, I feel a hand on my shoulder. And then that hand starts to weigh me down—no, it starts to *push* me down. I slip under the surface for a moment then shoot back up, my whole body locking up.

"Tommy, listen to me. I need you to let her go," Shane says calmly but firmly. "Tommy, *please*. You're panicking. Let me get her out, and then I'll get you, okay? It'll only be a sec. Tommy!"

But then I feel his hand on me again, pulling me down, pushing me out of his way. I look at Tommy's face, and I don't recognize him. There's nothing left but blue skin and panic. No trace of him.

"Tommy! *Fuck!*" Shane calls. He shimmies to the other side and crawls to my left, then chucks the branch back out so that it's out of Tommy's reach but in mine. "Jules, reach out and grab that, okay?" Tommy flails behind me, but I reach the branch just in time. My hands are frozen, but I manage to grab onto it and hold with whatever mobility is left in them. And then suddenly, I'm not in the water anymore. But I can't move.

"Jules, hold onto the branch, okay? Just hold on. I've got you," Shane says, his voice calm despite everything. I close my eyes and clutch on, letting him drag me across the ice and snow. When he reaches me, he tucks his hands underneath my armpits and pulls me all the way off the ice and onto the shore.

I can't feel my face, and all I feel in my toes and fingers is a strange burning sensation. I lie on the ground, staring up at the stars, wondering how they can remain so calm and bright, just watching the scene below.

"Jules, hang on, okay? Just hang on..." I hear Shane say, but I can't keep my eyes open. My head feels heavy, and I'm not sure if I can even lift it.

"Jules! Goddamnit! Stay awake, Jules, stay awake!"

I can hear him calling to me like he's miles and miles away, searching for me in the night. I know he's close, but I can't see him. I can't feel him.

All I feel is the weight of the ice, the cold of the water, pulling me further and further down.

I OPEN MY EYES SLOWLY, blinking several times before my vision clears. The fluorescent lights in the hospital room make it feel like I'm on a stage, like all eyes are on me. And when I look around the room, I realize that's true.

My mom is on my right, scooted as close to the bed as her chair will let her. I see Luna in the back corner, pacing back and forth. Kirby is next to my mom, standing behind her chair, and my Aunt Ruby is behind them.

To my left, sitting in a chair with his face in his hands, is my very best friend. The one who just saved my life. The one who pulled me and Tommy…

I can't remember everything. I remember the cold. So, *so* fucking cold. I remember him holding me in the cab of his truck after he had called 911. I remember him rocking me back and forth, holding me against his bare chest and turning all the heat vents toward me, rubbing my arms. I remember him crying into my hair, whispering to me that I would be okay.

And then I remember him telling me he was sorry.

Sorry for what?

Then, the flashing of the red and blue came, and I knew I could rest a little bit. That my Shane had taken care of me. That I was going to be okay.

"Sweetie," my mom says, her voice breaking as she reaches out to take my hand. "You're awake." Tears are already streaming down her face as she scoots in even closer, taking my hand in both of hers and squeezing it.

"How ya feelin'?" Aunt Ruby asks, leaning in closer to me. "You gave us quite a scare."

I swallow then try and focus on my body. I actually feel okay. There's a heated blanket on top of me, but I wiggle my toes beneath it, and they all seem to still be there. I squeeze Mom's hand and wiggle the fingers on the other. I feel tired, like I've been through hell and back.

But maybe that's because I have been.

"I feel okay," I say, my voice a little hoarse. "How long have I been here?"

"About eight hours or so, hon," Mom says. "I'm so glad you're okay."

She leans forward and kisses the side of my head, rubbing my shoulders.

"I'm sorry, Mom," I say, my own lip starting to quiver. I hate seeing her hurt over me. "I didn't mean to... Tommy was just excited, and—" I pause and look around, scanning every person in the room.

"Where is he?" I ask. The room grows quiet, and Mom covers her mouth with her hand, closing her eyes. I look from one person to the next, but they all look away or down at the ground. And then my eyes land on Shane again. His eyes are trained on mine, like he's willing me to understand before he has to speak it. Finally, he stands up and walks to the bed, sitting on the side of it. He takes my hand in his and clears his throat.

"Do you guys mind giving us just one minute?" he asks them barely above a whisper. Mom nods and kisses me again. She rubs Shane's back then follows the rest of them out of my room.

"What's going on, Shane?" I ask, afraid for the answer. My brain is scrambling to remember the last few minutes before the ambulances arrived.

He's looking down at our clasped hands resting on his knee, but my eyes are searching him. Every inch of his face, every bit of the pain behind his eyes. I reach up and let my fingers drag across a scrape on the side of his face.

"What happened?" I ask. Slowly, he reaches his hand up and presses it against mine on his cheek.

"I scraped it on the ice," he says. "Jules, I have to tell you something."

I drop my hand, my heart rate accelerating in my chest.

"By the time I had gotten you out," he says between a series of long breaths, "the ice had cracked more." He pauses for a minute then starts again. "When I went back to get Tommy, he was…"

His voice trails off again, and he squeezes his eyes shut. Then I feel the wetness of a single tear on my hand, and he swipes it away with his thumb.

"Shane," I whisper, taking my hand from underneath his and putting it on his other cheek. "Tell me what happened."

"He was gone," he says. More tears stream from his eyes, falling down his cheeks, soaking into the sheets and my skin. "I looked everywhere; I even tried to get back out to the hole where you first went in, but the ice cracked too much that I couldn't even get out a few feet."

I lean back against the pillow and close my eyes.

"They sent in a dive team since the ice was so thin," he goes on. Then he pulls his hands from mine and drops his head. "They found him about an hour ago. I'm so sorry, Jules. I'm sorry I couldn't—"

His voice cracks, and he covers his face with his hands.

I want to sob, to scream, to cry out for both of them. I want to help Tommy, pull him out with me. I want to hold Shane.

I can only do one of those things right now. I push myself up and wrap my fingers around his arms, pulling him onto the bed.

"Hey, hey," I whisper, pulling his head to my shoulder and stroking the back of his hair. "It's okay.

We're okay. You got me out of there. I'm here because of you."

We're quiet for a few moments, holding each other close, my shoulder wet from his tears, and his shoulder wet from mine. He pulls away slowly and wipes them on his sleeve, his beautiful sapphire eyes covered in a red haze.

"Look at me," I tell him, and he does. "This is not your fault."

His eyes drop again, and I use my finger to tilt his chin.

"*Look at me,*" I command again. And much more slowly this time, he does. "You saved my life tonight."

He takes my hand in his and presses it to his lips.

"But I couldn't save you both," he whispers. I pull him into me again, and he pulls his legs up onto the bed. He curls in next to me, and I turn into his chest, breathing him in, letting his heartbeat drown out the noise of all the beeping machines and blinking lights around us. Tears roll from my eyes onto his shirt, tears for Tommy, tears for Shane. Tears for me.

As Shane slowly drifts off to sleep, I lie awake, the finality of everything that has happened in the last few hours hanging heavily around me. I'll never see Tommy again. He'll never pull me in for a hug; he'll never be next to me at the rest of Shane's meets. He'll never carry me around on his back or onto the ice. We'll never spin around in circles, celebrating our milestones. He'll never visit Shane and me in California. He'll never have a next step.

And then I look at the sleeping boy before me. The boy who is almost a man.

Gosh, when did that happen?

I think it happened eight hours ago, out there on that lake. I run my hand lightly down his cheek, tracing his jawline with my thumb, Tommy's last words to me before our whole world came crashing down beating me in the brain.

You're amazing, Jules. And that guy, he thinks it, too. And I don't know if he's ever gonna tell you. So I'm telling you.

And as I watch him breathe in and out, one arm draped over my hip, the other tucked under my head, I realize I don't want to waste more time. If I've learned anything from the last eight hours of my life, it's that time is something we are constantly running out of, and I don't intend to waste any more of it.

I push myself closer to him and lean up, leaving a soft kiss on the warmth of his cheek.

I need him, and he needs me.

It's time I stop letting the fear of losing him stop me from the joy of having him.

I BLINK WILDLY in the sunlight that streams in from the window of my hospital room, and the first thing that comes into focus is Kirby. She's sitting in the chair to my left, where Shane had been sitting the night before.

"Morning, sunshine," she says, closing the magazine she was reading and setting it down on the side table.

"Moms are getting us breakfast from the cafeteria. The nurse is coming back to check your vitals again, and if all looks okay, you'll be discharged later this morning," she says, leaning her elbows on the bed. I smile and nod.

"Thanks, Kirb," I tell her. "Where's Shane?"

She tilts her head, giving me a strange look.

"Shane?" She looks around and shrugs. "He wasn't here when we got here this morning."

I lie back on my pillow and stare up at the tray ceilings.

Did I dream it all?

I look around for my phone but remember it had been in my back pocket when we went down.

"Can you text him for me? I just want to make sure he's doing okay. And let him know I'll be leaving soon," I ask. She nods.

"Sure thing."

Mom and Aunt Ruby are up with breakfast in the next few minutes, and my nurse and doctor are in shortly after. Before I know it, I'm back at home, lying in my own bed. My phone had been in my pocket when we went down, so it's unusable. Kirby comes in to bring me a bowl of soup, and I sit up.

"Thanks, Kirb," I tell her as I take the tray. "Um, has Shane…?"

She shakes her head slowly.

"Nope, nothing yet," she says. "I'm sure he's probably just decompressing at home, ya know?"

I nod.

It's been almost two weeks, and there's been no sign of Shane. My new phone hasn't come in yet, and he hasn't responded to anyone's texts. If Mom wasn't withholding my car keys and basically forbidding me to leave her sight, I would be over there in a second.

I'm lying back on my bed, flipping through channels, when Mom appears at my bedroom door. She looks somber, like someone has just died.

Well, someone *else.*

"Sweetheart, Mrs. Hunter is here," she says. I immediately perk up, pushing my tray off my lap.

"Mrs. Hunter? Is Shane with her?" I ask. Mom shakes her head.

"No, hon. She wants to talk to you. But listen, if you're not up for it, if you just need some rest, I'll ask her to come back."

I shake my head.

"No, no," I say. "Send her in."

Mrs. Hunter looks as classy as always, even in her jeans and sweatshirt. Her hair is pulled back in a perfect bump, and though she's wearing a little less makeup than usual, she still has the remnants of some on her face.

"Hi, honey," she says, a sad smile crossing over her lips. She holds up a gift bag. "Brought you a little something…for later."

I nod. She leans down to hug me, and I inhale her familiar perfume, the remnants of the Hunter house smell on her clothes. She sits down in front of me and pats my hand.

"I'm so glad you're alright," she says, looking into my eyes.

"I have Shane to thank for that," I say back. "Is he okay? He was gone when I woke up at the hospital, and I've had some trouble getting a hold of him."

She nods slowly then looks back down at our hands.

"Jules, Shane has made the decision to graduate early. Since he already has his credits, he will actually be graduating in just a few weeks. Just as you have, I'm sure, Shane has really been struggling with everything that's happened. We will be leaving after Tommy's funeral tomorrow to take him out to L.A. The swimming coach was able to help us find him an apartment, and he will actually start classes in the spring semester."

I stare at her, watch her lips move, but I can't seem to make sense of anything she's saying.

We're going together.

We're supposed to be going together.

I see tears forming in the corners of her eyes.

"You have been such an amazing friend to him, sweetheart," she whispers, rubbing my hand. "I wish it were different, but he's got to do what he's got to do to heal. And as much as I want to force him to...as much as I think he should be here himself, I've got to be his mom and look out for what will help him get better."

My eyes stay wide.

She's saying he's not coming.

She's saying he's not coming because he doesn't want to speak to me.

"I'm so sorry, honey," she says, standing up at my bedside and kneeling down to kiss my head. "You were truly the best friend he ever had."

The past tense gives me the chills. She turns and leaves slowly, and I roll onto my side to digest everything.

He's leaving to live the life we talked about.

He's leaving me after everything that's happened.

He's leaving me after I realized that I'm in love with him.

I loved him, and I lost him.

20

He clenches his hands to stop the trembling.

"So, it wasn't just that you could only get to one of us…" I whisper, the missing pieces all filling in.

He shakes his head.

"It's that I could have gotten either of you, and I made a choice to get you first. I saved one friend, but in turn, I killed another."

My heart is rising up into my throat. No wonder he ran. It wasn't just guilt over only being able to help one of us. It was the shame of choosing *which one* it was. It was the weight of the responsibility of making a choice at seventeen of which friend lived and which friend died.

"Shane, you didn't…"

"I'm sorry. I'm sorry I left, and I'm sorry I didn't say anything. But when I looked at you in that hospital bed, I don't know… I guess the thought of living out this awesome life—and with you, no less—felt like I was choosing to let him die all over again."

I swallow.

"But when I got back here a few months ago, and I saw you at the resort that night, I realized…" His voice trails off for a minute. "I realized Tommy would have kicked my ass for leaving you the way that I did." A sad smile crosses both of our lips. His eyes meet mine, and he goes on. "And I realized that I'd do it all over again. I'd do anything to save you, Jules. Over and over again."

I can't remember the last eleven years. I don't remember the hurt. I just feel him. I reach out and grab his face, pulling him in closer and letting my lips brush against his. He tastes like I always imagined he would—like everything I've ever missed.

But as he goes to break the kiss, I pull him in harder. I've waited too long to taste him, and I'm not ready to stop. I let my tongue slide between his lips, finding his and tasting him further. He moans, and I can feel the match lighting at my very core.

I lean back against the step and pull him onto me by the collar of his coat. He lets his hands slide up my back, and the other slides from my cheek into my hair, holding my head where he wants it so that his mouth can take what's his.

"Jules," he whispers between kisses. When we come apart for a breather, I open my eyes and look at him.

"Come inside," I whisper. He narrows his eyes on mine, his lips twisting up into a devious smile.

"Jules, you sure?" he asks. I push him off of me and stand up, then I grab his collar and pull him in for another hot, long kiss. When I come away from him, I suck his bottom lip between my teeth for a minute before letting him go.

You can take that as a firm "yes," Mr. Hunter.

He follows me in through the door and closes it, and for a moment, we both stare at each other. I reach down to slide my sweatshirt over my head, and he shimmies out of his jacket. Then, I rush to him, like these last twenty seconds of not touching have been too much to bear. I wrap my arms around his neck, kissing his lips, his jaw, and slipping down to his neck. I suck and bite at it, leaving little flicks with my tongue. The scent of his skin is driving me wild, and I don't want to wait anymore. More than a decade is long enough.

"Damn, Jules," he says before wrapping his hands around my waist and lifting me up. I wrap my legs around him as he walks toward the counter, setting me down. I clench my thighs around him, pulling him into me, and I can feel how hard he is through his jeans. I grind myself against him slowly, agonizingly, while my tongue continues to taste him. He growls as our bodies seem to lead the way, and he reaches down for the hem of my t-shirt, throwing it up over my head and onto the floor. I do the same with his sweater, tossing it across the room, and I feast my eyes on his chest—the Shane Hunter 2.0 version. The version where you took teenage perfection and added a little *more* perfection to it. Strong and wide, the curves of his muscles, the deep, defined ridges of his abs. They tease me, all pointing down, leading me to the V at the top of his pants.

"Damn," I say as I lean forward to kiss his chest, "you've aged well." He chuckles as he leans me back, his eyes scanning my navel, up to my cleavage, before finding mine. His hands are soft and gentle across my skin, leaving a trail of burning want in their wake. They make their way around my back to my bra strap and skillfully unclasp it. Without breaking our insatiable kisses, he hooks his fingers under the straps and slides it off of me then pauses to take me all in.

"I could say the same about you," he whispers before crashing his lips against mine again, his hands cupping my breasts, his fingers gently tugging my nipples.

He slides me off the counter and carries me down the hall.

"Bedroom," he says between kisses as we swirl around in circles.

"Next door on your right," I tell him as we reach it. He throws open the door and carries me to the bed, laying me down gently. He kisses my hip, my stomach, and up to my chest before taking my nipple into his mouth, swirling it around with his tongue. He slides up to my neck, his lips finding their way up my jaw and to my mouth. He runs his fingers through my hair, cupping my head as his mouth makes love to mine. I slide my hands up to the top of his jeans and undo them, tugging them down over his boxers. He kicks them away and reaches for the waistband of my sweatpants then pauses.

"Jules," he breathes, "are you sure you want this?"

I push myself up onto my elbows, practically panting.

"Why would I not want this?"

"I just want to make sure it's *this* Jules that wants it. Not the old Jules." I look up into his big, gray-blue eyes, hot with the same fire that's burning in me but also filled with worry.

"Maybe this is for *that* Jules," I say, "but let's let her have it."

I tug him back down to me for another kiss then lie back on the bed. He looks at me for a moment then gives in, reaching to tug my sweatpants off. He slips one finger in through the side of my panties, and I let out a sharp breath, arching my back and pushing my head into the mattress.

"My God, Jules," he whispers, sliding his fingers across the wetness that's already there. He slowly slides my panties down off my legs then reaches up and tugs his boxers off, letting himself spring free. I feast my eyes on him—*all* of him—taking in what I've been deprived of for so long. He crawls back up my body, kissing my calf, my inner thigh, and the crease of my leg. His eyes flick up to mine, then he runs his tongue over my folds once, then twice, before sliding a finger deep inside of me, then another.

I clench onto the sheets, pushing myself backward more, but he puts his other hand on my stomach to hold me down, keeping me where he wants me. He works them in and out, feeling my depth, like he's trying to learn his way around. He slowly slides them out then reaches down for his pants on the floor, tugging the tiny square package from his pocket. He looks up at me as he starts to roll the condom on.

"Just so we're clear, I always keep one of these in my pocket," he says. "I wasn't, uh, expecting anything, coming over here."

"Oh, so, you always have one? Just because there's *always* a chance some girl's gonna wanna sleep with you?" I ask, my lips curving up into a mischievous smile. He shakes his head.

"N-no, that's not what I meant, either. I'm just always, uh, prepared, and I—"

"Shane," I say, spreading my legs apart and letting my hand slide down between my breasts, over my belly button, and rest on my center. "I've been waiting to do this for a long time. Now *I'm* the one expecting something. So come here."

He swallows as he eyes my hands, slowly maneuvering the area where I crave him so badly.

He climbs onto the bed and leans down to kiss and lick me again, priming me for the main entertainment. He crawls up the length of my body so that we're chest to chest, nose to nose, then he pushes into me so hard that I scream out.

He moves back and forth, slowly at first while he's finding his place, learning the angles that make my eyes roll back. When he finds his rhythm, he picks up his pace, over and over, back and forth, straight and angled thrusts that make me dig my nails into the skin of his back.

"Fuck, Shane," I moan underneath him. He slides his hands down and wraps them around my legs, pulling them farther apart. He slows down a little, but I clench myself around him and dig my nails in more. "Don't stop."

He smiles.

"Yes, ma'am," he says. But to my surprise, he pulls out of me and slides off the bed onto his feet. He grabs my legs and yanks me down to the edge of the bed, then he throws one of my legs up onto his shoulder. Then, he dives back into me, one hand around my leg, one hand circling my center as he moves.

"Oh, God, Shane," I whisper, biting my lip and closing my eyes. He's hitting a spot that I didn't know was inside of me, and I can feel my body starting to tremble beneath him.

"Come for me, Jules," he growls, his thrusts getting

harder, deeper. I open my eyes to look at him, and the carnal gaze in his throws me.

"Oh, God…"

"That's it, Jules," he says. "That's it…"

Then it happens, exploding through me from my core to my extremities until I'm a sweaty, panting mess. He lets himself go a second later, letting out one final moan as he lowers himself on top of me.

I wrap my arms around his neck, pulling him into me, the sweat from our bodies making our skin stick together. He kisses me softly then pulls up to look at me. He pushes a piece of my hair out of my face with his finger then tilts my chin up again for one more.

He cleans himself up in the bathroom and comes back out just as I'm reaching for a shirt in my dresser. But as I pull it out, he turns me around to face him then takes me in his arms and kisses me again.

He lifts me up and carries me to the bed, and for a moment, I think he's going for round two.

He lies down on top of me, resting his chin on my bare chest.

"I wanna stay with you tonight," he whispers. I swallow and run my fingers through his thick hair.

"I'd like that," I whisper back.

"But on one condition," he says, that mischievous look that I'd recognize from a mile away appearing in his eye.

"What?"

"We sleep naked," he says. I laugh and shove him off of me, crawling up to the top of the bed and pulling down the covers.

"That can be arranged."

21

I wake up to the smell of bacon and an empty bed. I slip out and pull on an oversized t-shirt and walk out to the kitchen.

"Morning," he says, wearing nothing but his jeans at my stove. Forget whatever he's cooking; I just want him for breakfast.

"Morning," I say sleepily, trudging over to pull up a stool at the counter in front of him. "I had bacon?"

He laughs.

"Nope," he says. "I ran out to the market this morning. I get up early these days." He slides me over the hot chocolate he got me and gets back to work, making the bacon.

"Wow, that's a change," I tell him. "The only time you used to get up early was if you were swimming."

"Yeah, well. You miss half the day if you sleep in," he says. Now, I laugh.

"You sound like an old person," I tell him. "And sometimes it's okay to miss half the day." I reach across the counter and snag a piece of done bacon off the plate that's next to him. He finishes the last piece and turns off the stove, then he scoops some scrambled eggs from a pan into a bowl. He holds them up.

"I was gonna make you breakfast in bed, but it seems like you didn't want to stay in bed," he says.

"Oh, I wanted to stay in bed," I say, scooting off the stool and walking to the table, "but I wanted something *else.*"

He sets the plate and the bowl down on the table and lifts his eyes to me, his lips parting a little.He looks back down with a shy smile and shakes his head.

"Jules," he says, "I, uh, last night was amazing."

Heard this one before.

"Last night was amazing, but I'm not looking for anything serious right now."

"Last night was amazing, but I'm not really looking for a commitment."

"Last night was amazing, but…"

I snag another piece of bacon and look up at him.

"But?" I offer.

"Last night was amazing, but I don't want you to get the wrong idea," he says. Ahh, the wrong-idea excuse. Haven't gotten that one in a while. "I didn't come up here just to…just to do that and then leave. I mean, what I'm saying is, I didn't come up here for that at all. I came here because I missed you. I came here because I wanted to fix things, and I…" His voice trails off, and it's so endearing how nervous he is right now. Within a matter of weeks, we've found our footing as friends again. But within the last few hours, we've crossed a whole new line, into totally foreign territory, whether we had remained friends over the last decade or not.

"What you're saying is, you didn't come over last

night just to fuck me and then dip?" I ask with a smile. He startles at my bluntness and then smiles.

"Yeah, I guess that's what I'm saying," he says. He walks around the table to where I'm standing and puts his arms around me, clasping the table on either side. He leans in close so that he's in my hair.

"But I didn't fuck you last night."

I turn so that we're facing each other and narrow my eyes at him.

"Oh, you didn't?"

He leans in and takes my lips with his, showing off how well he knows his way around them.

"No," he says when we break. "You'd know if I fucked you."

Butterflies rush around my stomach.

"Then what was last night?"

He sighs and pulls back, turning toward the window and looking out at the snow.

"Last night was...beautiful." He turns his head to me slowly, and I smile and walk toward him, wrapping my arms around his neck and pulling him in for another long, slow kiss.

We finish eating breakfast and clean up, and I get dressed into some real clothes and come back out. He's back in his clothes from last night, and I can't help but smile.

"What?" he says.

"Nothing. I just never thought Shane Hunter would be doing the walk of shame from my house."

He shakes his head and throws a couch pillow at me.

"So, what do you have going on the rest of the weekend?" he asks.

"Well, I have a pick-up tomorrow for a birthday party, but then nothing else."

"What about tonight?" he asks. I smile.

"What about tonight?"

"Well, I know Derrick and Kaylee had mentioned having some people over, and I wanted to see if you were going. I can pick you up."

I nod, my back turned to him as I put the last of the dishes away. *What does this mean? What does any of this mean?*

I turn back to him, the dish towel tucked up into my fist.

"Let me ask you something," I say. "What's the latest with the promotion? And the land?"

He swallows, and his eyes grow wide.

"Reed hasn't, uh, given me much to work with yet. We're still looking. I won't know about the promotion for another few weeks."

"Uh huh," I say, walking toward him.

"So, in another few weeks, you could get that promotion and waltz on back to the west coast, right?" I ask.

His Adam's apple bobs again. He nods.

"It's possible."

I look him up and down, remembering how amazing his body looks naked, how every muscle flexed while he moved inside of me, how his strong arms moved me around like I weighed nothing.

"Then I guess we should make the best of the next few weeks. Right, *friend?*"

He almost cringes and gives me a strange look.

"Right," he mutters, one eyebrow still raised.

I know what he's thinking. No two friends can look

at each other the way we do, take each other the way we do, crave each other the way we do. But in a few weeks, this reunion could be all over. Back to living without him. So, friends it is. Friends-with-benefits is to be determined.

Last night was amazing, Hunter. But I can't let you leave me again.

22

"Why are you riding with him?" Kirby asks me over the phone as I flick on some mascara in the bathroom mirror.

"Because he offered to pick me up."

"How does he know where you live?"

I swallow.

Because he was inside of my house...and me...last night.

"Uh, I had to give his mom my address for the invitations," I say quickly, relieved with my quick response.

"Hmm," she says suspiciously. "I smell a lie."

"What are you talking about?"

"I can sense it. It's in your voice," she says. "You don't seem as...cold toward him."

I pause.

"I'm not," I admit.

"What changed?"

"We...talked."

"You did? When?"

I cringe and squeeze my eyes shut. I cannot lie to her. I cannot.

"Last night," I mutter.

"Last night? At his party?"

"Uh, no. He, uh, stopped by."

There's a long pause.

"You slept with him, didn't you?" she asks.

"Oh my *God!* How do you do it? How can you tell?" I blurt out. She laughs.

"You're a terrible liar, and you're terrible at hiding things. Always have been," she says. I groan.

"Are you gonna scold me now and tell me to stay away?" I ask.

"No," she says. "You're a grown-ass woman. You can do with your own hoo-hah whatever you please. I'd love to warn you and then say I won't be here to pick up the pieces, but we both know that's not true. If you let him, he might hurt you again. But only you know if that'll be worth it or not. So, whatever you decide, I will begrudgingly be here to dry your tears and curse his name all over again," she says. I smile.

"I love you, Kirb."

"I know, I know. See ya tonight."

I WALK BACK out to my closet and sort through the outfits I pulled aside. I haven't given this much thought to what I wanted to wear in a long time. As I'm deciding between my skinny jeans that cut off my circulation or a stretchy pair of yoga pants, there's a knock at the door. I look at my phone.

He's early.

I rush out and open it.

"Sorry, I'm not quite ready," I tell him. "You can

come in and watch some T.V. while I finish, if you want."

But I see his eyes starting at my bare feet, moving up my legs to the single white towel that's covering me, tied at my chest. My damp locks bellow down my shoulders, and I realize I'm basically naked. I clear my throat and tug the towel up some. Finally, his hooded eyes meet mine.

He steps inside, and I close the door. The dark-blue shirt he has on makes his eyes pop, and I'm losing the battle of not wanting to jump him again.

"I'll be right out," I tell him as I walk back toward my bedroom.

"I think you should wear that," he says. I freeze at my doorway and turn back to him slowly. I tug at the top of the towel, letting it loosen and fall off.

"Maybe I'll go like this, instead," I say, my voice low and husky. I feel that heat in my most sensitive parts, the dampening between my legs, my naked chest heaving up and down. His eyes widen, and I can see the feeling is mutual.

"You might want to put that back on," he warns. I raise an eyebrow.

"Why?"

"Because in a minute, the way I'm going to touch you is not exactly how one *friend* would touch another."

I bite my lip.

"Then maybe we're not friends right now," I say. He wastes no time walking toward me, wrapping his arms around my waist and pulling me into him. He bites my bottom lip gently and tugs my hair with one hand while the other slips down between us. He delves in, playing me like a violin, making my body shake and shudder with every move of his fingers. But before I can say anything, he drops to his knees in front of me.

"What are you doing?" I ask.

He looks up at me, the look in his eye devilish and ravenous.

"Not being your friend," he says, pushing my legs apart. He pushes up and licks the entire length of my folds, clenching onto my ass and pushing himself further into me. I grab onto the door frame with a yelp, steadying myself as the stars start to appear in front of my eyes.

"Oh, shit, Shane," I whisper, my head dropping back. I lean back slightly, but he grabs my ass harder, holding me in place.

"Where are you goin'?" he asks. I look down at him and smile, biting my lip as I wait for the rest. His hand slides up to my breast, circling it, squeezing it in sync with his tongue below, and my legs turn to jelly beneath me. "God, you taste amazing."

"Jesus Christ," I stammer, locking my legs. I feel myself getting closer to the edge and reach out to grab hold of his hair as his head twists and turns, his tongue dancing across me, in me, his moans sending vibrations through my whole body. "Shane," I mutter. "Shane, I…"

I stomp my foot, clenching every muscle as the orgasm rips through my body. He licks his lips as he stands, looking down at me as I catch my breath, my chest glistening with sweat. He presses his body against mine, and I can feel his hardness. He's ready, and so am I. I'm half tempted to lie down on this floor and spread my legs. I want more, and he knows it.

Slowly, a smile spreads across his lips as he leans in next to my ear.

"You need to get dressed," he whispers, and my jaw drops. No way. No way is this over.

"Why?"

"Because we're gonna be late. I'll meet ya out here." Then, casual as ever, he nudges me into my room and winks, closing the door behind him.

And I stand there, butt-ass naked, standing in the remnants of my newfound-ex-best friend going down on me.

The whole way to the party, I don't say anything. I sit in the passenger seat with my arms crossed, a pout on my lips. He's chuckled at me a few times, trying to get me to lighten up, but I'm dedicated to this act right now. I carry in the extra cupcakes I made at work yesterday, and he opens the door like the freakin' perfect gentleman he is.

"Hey, J," Derrick says as he puts a cheese platter down on the huge dining room table. He kisses my cheek as he reaches for the cupcakes then pauses when he sees Shane right behind me. "Oh, hey, Shane. You guys, uh, come together?"

Shane and I look at each other for a second, and I clear my throat.

"Uh, yeah. Shane offered to pick me up," I say. "Like old times."

Shane smiles.

"Not *exactly* like old times," he says under his breath, and I stare at him, wide-eyed, as

Derrick walks past, totally oblivious. Shane chuckles

as I elbow him in the ribs, following Derrick out to the huge great room where everyone else is already sitting.

I kneel down to hug Luna. I kiss the top of Kirby's head. And Kaylee is already trying to fix me a drink.

"Want a Shirley Temple?" she asks sweetly. I nod.

"That would be great," I say. My mom hasn't had a drink in over ten years, but I'm not taking any chances. She drank to forget, and I want to remember.

After a few minutes of catching up, Kaylee stands and walks slowly to the back door.

"Oh my gosh, guys, it's snowing!" she says, clapping her hands. We all chuckle. Kaylee is from the south, so she still gets as excited as a school kid praying for a snow day.

"Should we go out?" Derrick asks, walking up behind her and wrapping his arms around her.

"Yes!" she says, breaking out of his clutch and running to the coat rack. "Football!"

We all laugh and stand, slowly getting our layers on like reluctant parents who know they're going to have a backache the next day. I pull my coat on, but I know I'm not dressed for this. Shane smiles.

"Ya know, I, uh, have a hoodie you can borrow in my car," he says. I can't help but grin.

"I'll take it."

He jogs out and grabs it, bringing it back up to me on the porch. I tug the soft cotton on over my head then put my coat back on top and follow him around the back of the house. Derrick and Ryder are picking teams, and despite Ryder not being able to make out much of anything in the dark, he seems ecstatic to play.

"I'll be permanent quarterback," he says, "so you all might want to be loud if you're open!"

I get picked on Derrick's team, and Ryder takes Shane. Just like old times, we line up across from each other, and I spin the ball of my foot into the slick grass to gain my footing. Everything will be covered in white soon, making Meade Lake the picturesque little town that looks great on a postcard. Mila is laughing at something Luna said, and Kaylee is jumping up and down excitedly. Kirby is bitching about having to be out in the cold unnecessarily, and I can't help but smile.

"I'm comin' for you, Grey," he whispers.

"Good luck," I whisper back with a smile just as the ball is hiked. I take off, breezing past him and weaving in and out of the unsuspecting other team. Derrick launches the ball to me, and I jump up and catch it, landing gracefully on my feet and running for the goal line. I feel hands grab around my waist, but I'm determined to make every move count. I cross the line just as Shane wrestles me to the ground, and the rest of my team cheers. He rolls around so he's on top of me, pinning me to the ground.

"You've gotten better," he says. I laugh.

"Guess you're not the only one with some surprise moves." I wink before shoving him off and jogging away.

Our team wins in a blowout, and we laugh and stomp the snow off our shoes as we walk back into the house.

"Guys, I think we're gonna take off before the roads start to get covered," Mila says. "Don't want to leave Alma with Annabelle for too long."

Derrick laughs.

"Aww, you know she'd keep that little girl for as long

as you'd let her," he says. "But go ahead and get your girl. And tell Mama I said hi."

"Yeah, I'm gonna head out, too," Kirby says. "No sleeping on couches for me anymore. Thanks for everything, guys."

The rest of us stand, clean up our trash, and head for our coats.

"You ready?" Shane asks. I nod. We say our good-byes and get back into his rental car.

"You sure this thing can handle a Meade Lake snowstorm?" I ask him with a smile. He shrugs.

"Guess we'll find out."

As we pull out of Kaylee and Derrick's neighborhood and onto Lake Shore Highway, we pass the strip mall where Marge's is.

"Shit!" I yell out. He stomps on the brakes for a sec.

"What? You okay?" he asks.

"Yeah, I just forgot we have that pick-up tomorrow at the shop. Gonna have to leave early tomorrow morning to get through the snow and get them done."

He tilts his head.

"Unless you want to just do them right now?" he asks. I look at him questioningly.

"What will you do?"

"Help," he says with a shrug. I think for a moment. Getting the cupcakes done now will make it a lot less of a rush tomorrow to get in and open up. I nod.

"Let's do it."

When we get to Marge's, I use my key to open the shop door and quickly turn the heat up as we both shake off the cold. Once Meade Lake winters hit, they *hit*. I walk toward the back counter and go around it, pushing on the door.

"I work back here," I tell him. "You can sit up here at one of the tables, if you want." He gives me a devilish smile and shakes his head.

"And miss all the cupcake action?" he asks. I laugh, and he follows me into the back. I pull out the cupcakes that Marge and I made yesterday and put them on the counter. I pull the icing out from the fridge—Marge's secret recipe that only I am privy too—and reach above the counter for the tray of color dyes. I spoon the icing out into two bowls and grab the blue dye and the red dye.

"Three drops of blue in here," I direct him, "and one drop of red in here."

"Yes, ma'am," he says, rolling up his sleeves so that those delicious arms that were wrapped around me so tight are on display.

"Just one?" he asks. I nod.

"Yep. You're making pale pink. It's for a gender reveal."

"A what?" he asks.

"A gender reveal. Ya know, when someone's having a baby. Although, if this snow keeps up, the baby might be here before anyone gets the cupcakes."

I take out the giant cupcake that I had made and stuffed with pink candy.

"This one has the colored candy in it that will tell them what they're having," I explain. "The parents will cut into it, and the candy will spill out."

I instruct him to mix, and once the shades are right, I start icing. I grab another spreader and teach him how to spin the cupcakes so that the icing goes on evenly. I only have to fix two of them.

"Not so bad, for a first-timer," I tell him. He smiles, looking down at his work.

"This is kinda fun," he says, licking a little bit of icing off his finger.

"It is," I say with a dreamy smile as I meticulously ice the giant cupcake, back and forth between the pink and the blue icing.

"You really like this, don't you?" he asks. I nod.

"I do," I tell him. "Who would have thought, after all that talk about going out west and leaving it all behind, that I would have found what I wanted right here in Meade Lake?"

He leans back against the counter, and I feel his eyes on me, but I can't bring myself to look at him.

"Yeah," he whispers. "Who would have thought."

I feel the air grow tense, and I know his words carry a lot more meaning than mine did at first.

"Do you like it out there?" I ask him, and I feel butterflies start to swirl in my belly. I don't know if I want to know the answer to this.

"Yeah," he says, and as I suspected, I feel a wave of sadness. "But then I come back here, and I can't remember why I left. I mean, I do know why. I was...suffocating here. But the truth is, I'm not sure if I could really breathe better out there, ya know?"

"That's just the smog," I say with a quick smile, trying to derail the heavy conversation that I'm afraid is going to follow. But he just shakes his head.

"No, it's not, Jules," he says. "I've been thinking a lot about how different things would

have been if I had just waited for you. If I had talked to you, ya know?" I put my spreader down and turn to him.

"Yeah, I know," I say. "I thought about that a lot, too, at first. Every single day." His eyes drop to the ground, and he takes a step closer to me.

"I'm sorry, Jules," he whispers. I turn to him.

"You've said your sorries," I tell him, "and I get it now. I do. I don't want you to be sorry

anymore. I'm happy. I really am. Everything happens for a reason, and I'm glad things turned out the way they did."

"Everything?" he asks, his eyes pleading with me. But I can't do it. I can't give him the answer he wants to hear, even if I want to hear myself say it just as badly.

He's going to leave you again, Jules.

"Yep," I say matter-of-factly. "I'm all good. And look at you. Big promotion in the works.

You're kicking ass. I'm proud of you and everything you did with your life, Shane. And I know Tommy would be, too."

I turn back to the cupcake and add the last bit of icing then carefully place the rattle and bottle I made from fondant yesterday on top.

"Done?" he asks. I stand back and admire my work.

"Done," I tell him. He moves up behind me, looking down at them over my shoulder.

"They look great," he says. "But you missed a spot."

I look down at my hands and arms and onto the counter, but I don't see anywhere that I've missed. When I turn to look at him, he swipes a line of blue icing across my cheek with his finger then sucks it off his fingertip as our eyes meet.

"You jackass," I tell him as I slowly dip my finger into what's left of the pink icing. I move toward him slowly as he backs away, holding his hands up in a playful surrender. When I have him up against the wall, I pause for a moment. He cocks his head and raises an eyebrow, then I reach my finger up to his lips and swipe the icing across. He laughs, but I pull him down to me so that our faces are just centimeters apart. I lick the icing off of his mouth then lick my own lips as our eyes meet. His jump back and forth between mine as the air around us gets a little less playful.

"I believe I have some catching up to do," I tell him as I sink down to my knees. But as I drop, he catches my elbows and pulls me back up.

"Not here," he says. I give him a look.

"Why not here?"

He steps closer and grabs my ass, pulling me into him so our bodies are flush against each other.

"Because I'm going to want to fuck you, and I don't think I should do that in your place of work." I swallow and slowly push apart from him.

"Well, would ya look at that," I say, looking down at my pretend watch, "time to clock out."

I rush back hurriedly to pack up the cupcakes, carefully placing them in one of our travel containers, and clean up the rest of the icing. This is casual. Just some casual, sexually intense foreplay between two friends.

When he helps me put the last of the supplies away, we walk out the front door.

"Let's go," I tell him.

"Yes, ma'am."

23

I don't think I've ever wanted to physically jump on anyone as much as I do right now. I don't think I've ever craved someone, wanted to taste them, wanted to tear the clothes off their body as much as I want to do it to his.

We're silent as he pulls the car out of the lot and onto Lake Shore Highway, cruising nice and slow as the snow and wind whip around us. The roads already have a thin layer of snow on them, and his car skids a little bit just getting out of the lot.

The roads are almost empty—Meade Lakers know to steer clear until the plows get out. One too many cars have ended up in an embankment, stuck, or even dangerously close to sliding right on down to the lake.

We drive past Lou's and past Derrick and Ryder's shop, all closed up for the night while everyone waits to see how the storm is going to play out. We're still about two miles from my street, but it feels like he might as well be back in fucking California. Even though we're mere inches apart, it feels like he's miles away.

But as we go farther down the road, we start to skid more and more. He slows down almost to a stop.

"Ya know, I'm not so sure this thing will get up the mountain," he says. "Should we go to my parents?"

I whip my head to him and shoot him a look.

"They went out to the beach house this morning," he says with a knowing smile. "No one is there."

I lick my lips and nod.

"Let's do it," I say.

A few painfully slow minutes later, we're pulling into the Hunters' driveway. But unlike any other time I've been here before, I'd never pulled up to this house knowing I was going to sleep with someone here.

In fact, I pulled up knowing I wasn't.

We get out and walk up the porch steps, and he punches in the code on the lock and holds the door open for me. I take off my scarf and boots, and he throws my coat on a hook as he walks by.

"You want anything to eat or drink?" he asks as he juts a thumb awkwardly toward the kitchen. I narrow my eyes and walk toward him.

"Are you trying to stall?" I whisper, our lips just centimeters from each other now. His eyes drop to my tongue as it wets my bottom lip. His chest heaves with quiet breaths, heavier now as we stand so close.

"No," he whispers back. I tilt my head.

"You sure? Because it feels like maybe you're trying to take your sweet time," I say back. The corner of his mouth pulls up slightly. His eyes narrow in on mine as he reaches up to swipe a piece of hair from the side of my face.

"I want to take all the time in the world when it comes to you," he says. I swallow.

"Then do it."

He wraps his hand through my hair, pulling me into him for a hard kiss. He tugs at the hem of my shirt before pulling it off completely, and I scramble to help him undo my bra. He scoops me up and carries me to the table, laying me down against it as he ravenously takes my nipple into his mouth, circling and pinching the other as he does it. I arch my back, clutching onto the sides of the table as he kicks the chair away and grabs hold of me. I tear the shirt up over his head, still writhing beneath him as his fingers start to do work on me. But before it gets too far, before I'm completely out of commission, I want to taste him. I push up onto my elbows and gently push him back to slide off the table. I shove him against the wall behind him. Before he can stop me, I tug his jeans and boxers down to the floor and take him into my mouth. He gasps and puts his hands back on the wall over me, holding himself up.

"Jesus Christ, Jules," he whispers, his eyes closed as he drops his head. I move my head back and forth, taking him in as far as he will go. After a few more moments, he pulls me up, giving me a look.

"I owed you," I say with a grin. But he doesn't smile back. There's something in his eyes now that wasn't there before, something that I think he was trying to keep at bay. It's fire. It's an all-consuming, blinding desire, and the only reason I know is because I have it, too.

He pulls me up from the ground and pulls my neck to his lips, biting and sucking and nipping as his hand slides down between my breasts and into my panties yet again. His other hand hooks onto the side and tugs them down, then he slides his fingers over me, inside of me, gliding through the wetness that he's created. I reach a hand around and grip him tightly, and he grips my ass with his other hand.

"Jules," he warns, a strange look in his eye.

"Come on, Hunter," I tell him. "How do you fuck those L.A. girls?" The words are sour in my mouth, the thought of him inside of anyone else making me feel an intense jealousy I haven't felt in years.

He reaches down and grips my thighs, lifting me up and wrapping my legs around his waist. He carries me back toward the living room toward the big glass doors at the back. He sets me down and turns me around so that I'm facing the window and presses me up against them. The cold glass sends an electric chill through my body, but as soon as I feel his hand sliding up my inner thigh and feel him open me up, I forget about the cold.

"You want this?" he growls into my ear from behind.

"Yes," I breathe, my palms flat against the door as I spread my legs farther apart. He pulls my hair off my shoulder, leaving a trail of slow kisses across the back of my neck. Then he wraps his arm around my waist from the back and pushes into me. The force makes me yelp with pleasure, and he leans in closer.

"You sure?" he asks again.

"Yes," I say. "Fuck me, Shane."

"Yes, ma'am," he says, then a switch goes off. He moves faster and harder with each thrust, my body flush up against the glass. Thank God for tall trees and no neighbors, because this would be a sight to see from the outside.

He kisses the side of my neck, one arm wrapped around my waist, holding me where he wants me, the other hand pressed up against the door on top of mine. I moan with every moment, begging him for more.

After a few more moments, he spins me around to face him, his kisses hard and wet as he holds my face in his hands. I wrap my arms around his neck, shimmying myself up his body, holding my groin out a bit so he can find me again. His eyes roll back as he enters me again, and seeing the pleasure, seeing what he gets from my body, sends me into overdrive. I want him to forget those L.A. girls. I hate every other woman who has ever seen this, felt this, wrapped themselves around this man.

He is mine, and he always has been.

Except, he's only yours for tonight.

I clench myself around him, igniting a flame behind his eyes. He backs us up to a wall, flinging my legs over his arms. He holds me steady as he pounds into me, and I drop my head back against the wall.

"Jesus, Shane," I whimper.

"You okay?" he asks, breathy. Our slick bodies stick together wherever our skin touches.

"I'm good," I tell him.

"Good," he says before pushing off the wall and walking toward the steps. He takes them two by two until we're in his room, and all the while, he's still inside me. He pushes the door open and sets me on top of his dresser, fucking me like he's never fucked anyone in his whole damn life.

He slides me off after a minute and sets me on the bed, and for a moment, I'm surprised. Missionary just doesn't seem to go along with the other moves he's thrown my way tonight, but I'll take him any way he wants me. With a devilish grin, he grabs my ankles and flips me over to my stomach.

Ah, that's more like it.

"You ready?" he asks, pulling me back toward him so that my ass is in the air. He leans forward and cups my breasts from behind.

"Yes," I whisper, clutching onto the sheets in front of me as I brace for the feeling of pure euphoria that I know is coming my way. Slowly, he pushes into me then pulls me up so his chest is touching my back. With one hand, he turns my head to the side so he can kiss me between breaths while the other slides down my body to the part of me he has thoroughly owned tonight. And as he pushes in and out, his hand makes circles in sync, faster and faster.

"Shane," I moan, reaching a hand up to grip his hair.

"Yes," he whispers into my hair.

"Shane," I moan again.

"Come for me, Jules. Let me see you come undone," he commands.

And I do, right there in his hands, until I see nothing but tiny black stars. I lay my head back against his chest just as he comes hard, tightening his grip around me as he lays his head on my shoulder.

He slides out of me, leaving a trail of soft kisses across my shoulder blades as he slides off the bed. He cleans up in the bathroom as I lie on his bed, completely spent. I stare up at the vaulted ceilings I had slept under so many times as a teenager, next to him right here, and I smile.

After a minute, he comes back, and I'm aware that I probably look way too comfortable. I roll over to my side and pull the covers up so that I'm covered, as if he didn't just see me more naked than I've ever been with anyone else.

He lies down next to me and rolls to his side so we're facing each other.

"Been a long time since we've been in this bed together," he says with a boyish smile.

"I was just thinking that," I tell him.

"Although, all the fantasies I had about you when we were kids didn't *exactly* come close to that," he says with a chuckle. I smile and push up onto my elbow.

"You fantasized about us?" I ask. He shoots me a look.

"You mean did I fantasize about having sex with my hot best friend when I was a horny teenager?" he asks with a laugh that warms me up. "Duh."

I laugh and cover my face.

"And as soon as I saw her again, eleven years later, I fantasized about it all over again," he says with a seriousness in his voice that wasn't there a second ago. I clear my throat and drop my eyes from his. I turn toward the window and slide off the bed with the sheet wrapped around me, walking toward it. I look out the window at the snow falling in the moonlight and sigh.

"Well, I'm glad it came true for you," I say with a nervous laugh. "I'm sure it didn't compare to the models and actresses you've met out there, but not bad for Meade Lake," I say with a sarcastic shrug. He pushes off the bed and walks toward me until I feel him inches behind me.

"There's nothing about you that's anything like any girl out there," he says, tucking a piece of hair behind my ear as he lowers his lips to it. "And eleven years from now, I won't be thinking about any of them. Not the way I've thought of you for the last eleven years."

I close my eyes, letting his words wash over me, the perfect period at the end of the most perfect night of my life. But when I open them, I'm reminded of reality. We can't stay up in this bedroom forever.

"Well," I say after a brief silence, "do you think we should brave it?" I ask, nodding my head toward the window. He raises an eyebrow and scoffs.

"What?" I ask.

"You think after *that*, I'm taking you home?" he asks with a grin. I smile back, suspicious. He walks to his dresser and tugs a t-shirt from it, tossing it to me, then pulls one out for himself. And then, as we had so many times, we climb into the bed and pull the covers up, looking up at the ceiling and laughing as we talk about our families and our jobs, as if the last decade hadn't happened.

24

For the next few weeks, Shane and I keep up this flirty, friendly facade. Hanging with our friends during the evenings, him visiting me at work during the days, falling into my bed by night, and repeating it all the next day. Kirby now refers to him as my "friend with benefit," but while I don't say anything, I think that makes it seem cheap.

Don't get me wrong.

I *know* that's it. Friends. My best friend is back, and now we just happen to have occasional, earth-shattering, mind-blowing sex. That's it. There haven't been many developments on the deal he's working on yet, and whenever it comes up, he seems to dodge the question. But I'm not pushing, half because it's not my business, and half because I don't want to know the answer.

His parents have gone out of town for the week to beat the storm we're supposed to get this weekend, so he invited the crew over for beers and s'mores, just like old times. I'm in the Hunters' huge kitchen, standing over the sink, washing a platter as I look out the window where the guys sit huddled up around the fire. I stare at him dreamily, watch the way he lights up the circle, the way they've all fallen right back into step. Just like Shane and I. Like he never left. Like everything is just the way he left it.

But he did leave, and he will again.

"It's cool, seeing you two like this," Luna says from behind as she carries in a handful of empty beer bottles. I jump as I turn to face her.

"Like what?" I ask her, feigning innocence.

"Please," she says sarcastically, popping a carrot stick into her mouth as she leans against the counter. "Like we don't all know whose bed you're sleeping in tonight." My eyes widen. "It's just...I don't know, nice. It's good to see you with someone. And I'm happy that someone is Shane."

I feel flames licking at my cheeks.

"Shane isn't my 'someone,'" I say with a swift eye roll as I turn back to the sink. "We're just having fun while he's back. He will probably be leaving soon again anyway." I try to keep my voice cool and casual, fighting back the panic that has started setting in the moment I think about him leaving Meade Lake again.

"Has he said anything else about the deal?" she asks, and I can feel the worry in her voice. I swallow and shake my head.

"Not much," I say. "But I know he's trying really hard to find something else for his boss." She nods.

The rest of the crew come inside for a new game Kaylee brought, and per usual, Shane and I kick ass. He still knows me better than anyone else—even the people who have been with me every day for the entirety of the eleven years when he was across the country.

It's not that he knows everything I've done, what foods I've grown to like or dislike, or what shows I'm watching. It's that he knows *me*. He knows what I'll say before I say it; he knows how I will react to something before I do. He knows the ins and outs of Juliette Grey, and I know once he leaves, no one else will ever know me this same way.

Finally, everyone leaves, but not without plenty of jokes about how I'll be staying with him tonight, making both of our cheeks burn red long after they take off. I yawn and stretch as I close the front door and hug my arms around myself. It was a long week, and I'm tired. He tugs me to him and kisses me, long and soft.

Too long. Too soft.

Hard and fast, that's what's safest for him and me.

I push into him harder, nibbling at his lip, caressing his tongue with mine. But with a moan, he pulls back.

When I finally lift my eyes to his, he's already staring at me.

"What is it?" I ask. He blows out a breath and drops his head a bit.

"Jules, are we…" He starts to ask, looking for the right words. "Is this"—he motions to the space between us—"okay? Whatever this, uh, arrangement is? Is this okay?"

"What do you mean, 'arrangement'?"

"I mean, us, doing this kind of stuff together. I mean us sleeping together, and touching each other, and whatever else this is. I care about you, Jules, and I want us to make sure we have a clear head. I could be leaving in a few weeks. What does…what does this mean?"

I swallow.

"It means we're just two friends that reconnected," I say with a casual shrug. "And that's all it needs to be."

I see instantly that my words have wounded him, but I can't fix it with more words. There's nothing else I can say without obliterating the progress, the growth I've had since he left the first time. So, I don't fix it with words. I'll fix it with my body.

"Jules," he whispers, wrapping his arms around me, "you're tired. And so am I. We actually can *just* sleep, ya know."

I swallow as I look up at him.

Just sleeping feels dangerous. Like this is getting to be more than just two friends who fuck.

"I can go home if you want?" I ask. But he rolls his eyes as he throws his arm around my neck and walks toward the steps. And as we settle into his bed, he pulls me close, and I realize how badly I did not want to go home and sleep alone.

I WAKE up a few hours later to a harsh vibrating sound coming from the nightstand next to me. Shane's arm is draped over my body, so I move as gently as possible to grab my phone before it wakes him up. But when I see it's three-thirty in the morning and it's Kirby calling, I slide out from under his arm and into the hallway.

"Kirb?" I mutter, squinting in the hall light.

"Jules," she says, her voice frantic and rushed. Very un-Kirby. "Where are you? I'm at your house, but no one's here."

"I, uh, I stayed at...I'm with Shane," I say quickly, expecting to have to jump on the defensive or deflect. But I don't have to do either. She doesn't even react.

"How fast can you get to your mom's?" she asks, and I can hear her trying to keep her voice calm.

"What is going on?" I ask her, my voice getting louder. "Kirby?"

Just then, I hear the bedroom door creak open, Shane standing in his boxers, rubbing his eyes in the light.

"It's your mom. She missed dinner with mine, and Mom just called me from her house," she says. "She's drunk, Jules."

My heart sinks into my stomach, and I stagger backward.

Drunk?

It's been more than a decade since she's had a drop of alcohol. She'd finally stuck to her guns. She'd finally done it for me. For us.

"What?" I whisper into the phone as the tears form and fall without worrying that he's standing right here, watching. Without hesitating, he reaches his arms out, pulling me into him.

"Is she…" My voice trails off.

"She's not hurt," Kirby says. "Lou happened to be driving home from the restaurant and saw her car crashed into a guardrail. Barely scratched the bumper, but she was passed out behind the steering wheel. We got her home, but she's really fucked up, Jules."

"Oh, my God," I whisper before bringing a hand up to cover my mouth. "I'll, uh, I'll get there as soon as I can."

I hang up and walk back into his room, gathering my things.

"What's going on?" he asks. "Everything okay?"

I shake my head as he follows me down the stairs, helping me grab my things as we walk.

"She's drunk," I say. His eyes widen.

"I thought you said she——"

"I thought so, too," I say, wrapping my arms around myself. "Do you think that car could get us to my mom's in this?"

He shakes his head.

"I won't chance it," he says, "but my dad's truck is in the garage. That'll get us anywhere."

When we get to my mom's, I practically jump out of the car and run into the house, heading for her bedroom without saying anything to Kirby. In her bedroom, she's puking into a bucket while Aunt Ruby holds her hair. When I walk through the door, Aunt Ruby looks at me, so much sadness in her eyes that it makes me sick.

"I'm sorry, baby," she says. "She was doing so well. We'll get her back on track, though."

I nod as I walk toward my mom, grabbing a fresh shirt out of her dresser on my way. When she's finally done puking, Aunt Ruby helps her drink some Gatorade while I run the shower. We help her in, and I hold her arm steady as she stumbles. We get her out and dressed, and Aunt Ruby pulls the covers down while Mom slips in without saying a word. She's on her side, and after a few minutes, Aunt Ruby motions toward the door.

"I think she's done now," she says. When we get out to the living room, Kirby is on the couch, watching T.V. Across the room sits my best friend, anxiously rubbing his knees until he sees us and stands.

"We got everything cleaned up," he says. "What else can I do?"

I look around at the spotless house in awe. I shake my head.

"There's nothing else," I say. "Thank you."

"Well, I'll stay with you," he says matter-of-factly. "And make sure she's good."

I think back to the first time he set foot in this house, on a night much like tonight. No judgment, no questions. Just doing everything he could to make sure the burden wasn't all on my shoulders. That was the first time I was truly vulnerable with Shane.

And this feels dangerously close to that.

I shake my head.

"No, I'm fine, really," I tell him. He raises his eyebrows.

"I'll stay with her," Kirby says from behind me, and I thank her silently for knowing what I need.

Kirby is my person. Luna is my person. *I* am my person. Shane can't be my person again. He looks from Kirby to me slowly then nods his head as he grabs his jacket.

"Okay," he says, an overwhelming sadness in his voice. "Call me if you need anything. Night, Kirb. Night, Ms. Broome," he calls to Aunt Ruby.

"Night," she and Kirby say in unison as they turn back to the T.V. I walk him to the door, and as he goes to leave, he turns back.

"You sure you don't need anything else?" he asks. I nod.

What I need I could never take from you again.

"I'm good," I tell him. "Goodnight."

. . .

LONG AFTER AUNT Ruby has left and Kirby has passed out on the couch, I'm sitting on the corner of my mom's bed, muffling cries into my knee as I watch her sleep.

THE NEXT MORNING, I wake up on the end of my mom's bed. Man, falling asleep in weird positions sure does fuck you up after the age of twenty-five. So unfair. I rub my eyes and roll over, and I find Mom sleeping peacefully. I sneak out of the room and take her car to the market to get some things that I know she'll need— sports drinks, soup, crackers, and bread. I get home and do a few loads of laundry then make the soup and pour some into a bowl around dinner time. I knock on the bedroom door and push it open slowly to find her already awake, just staring blankly ahead. When I walk in, she stirs gently.

"Hi, Mama," I whisper.

"Hi, baby," she whispers back.

"How do you feel?"

"Ha," she says as she sits up and leans against the headboard. "Like a fucking trainwreck."

I nod quietly.

"I guess we need to talk," she says. I nod and sit down on the bed, handing her the tray. She takes it with a sad smile but sets it on the nightstand next to her without eating.

"I guess so," I say. There's a long pause.

"First things first," she says. "I need you to know I have not had a drink in ten years up until last night. That's the God's honest truth."

I nod and let out a breath I didn't know I was holding.

"But the reason that I crashed last night…" she says, pausing to bite her trembling lip. She inhales sharply then opens her eyes again. "The reason I crashed last night is because I got a call from your Aunt Dawn."

Aunt Dawn is my dad's youngest sister and the only one on that side of the family who has kept in any sort of touch with us since he took off.

She leans forward and takes my hand, squeezing it as tears roll down her cheeks.

"Your daddy passed away yesterday of a heart attack, sweetie," she whispers as more tears roll down her cheeks. I don't react right away because I'm truly not sure how I feel. He left so long ago now that my emotions have sort of run their course. It's not that I forgave him, per se; it's just that I didn't have room for him anymore.

"Did you hear me, baby?" she asks. I clear my throat and nod.

"Yeah, uh, I, uh, yeah," I say. "I heard you." She nods.

"I want you to know that I'm going back to therapy, starting this week," she says. "And I've already checked in with my sponsor. This is the last time I drink over your father, baby. This is the last time I drink, period. I'm so sorry." She covers her mouth, her shoulders shuddering, and I lean across the bed and pull her into me.

"It's okay, Mama," I reassure her like I've done so many times. "It's okay. You and me, we're gonna be okay."

She cries harder, wrapping her arms around me tightly.

"I know your father and I had our shit," she says after she finally gets a hold of herself, "but you deserved better than that. You deserved better than that," she says again.

I hug her tightly.

"So did you, Mama."

She sighs and wipes the last tears from her eyes.

"Promise me, baby, that whenever you settle down, that you won't *settle* for anyone."

My eyes widen. I nod slowly.

"I promise."

WE LIE in bed for a while, holding hands and looking up at the sky through the single skylight in her bedroom as the flakes slowly cover it. Once she falls asleep, I slip out of her grip quietly, tug on my boots by the door, and get into my car.

25

The roads have a blanket of snow on them now, but it's nothing I've never driven in before. I pull into the Hunters' empty driveway a few minutes later, only his rental car parked near the back. I turn my car off and let out a long breath, but not long enough that I let myself change my mind. I hop out and practically run up the porch steps, banging on the glass. A moment later, he appears at the door, wearing nothing but baggy sweatpants and an unzipped sweat jacket. Heat pools in my core, and I bite my lip. He raises an eyebrow and opens the door.

"Jules?" he asks. "You okay?"

I don't say anything; I just spring forward, letting my lips crash into his, my arms wrapping around his neck, willing us to morph into each other. He lifts me off the porch and carries me into the house, closing the door slowly as he swings us around. He sets me down, gently breaking our kiss.

"Jules, you okay?" he asks again. I catch my breath and look up to him.

"My dad's dead," I say, and his eyes turn into saucers.

"Fuck," he breathes. "Do you, do you wanna talk—"

I shake my head and walk toward him again until we're chest to chest. I stand on my tip-toes and press my lips to his again, this time letting my tongue dance around on his. I press my groin into his, making him step back.

"No," I breathe. "I don't."

"Jules," he warns again, and I can feel my power taking over. A few more deep kisses, a few strokes of his hard length, and he'll be mine. He'll be mine to use; I'll be his to *be* used. Everything else can pause. He reaches up and unlocks my hands from his neck.

"Jules," he says more firmly this time. "We shouldn't do this right now."

"Why? We're friends, right?" I ask. He tilts his head to the side.

"Yeah, but—"

I step toward him again, tugging my shirt up over my head and pressing my breasts against his chest.

"And with friendship comes great benefits," I whisper. "Now, what was it you were saying the other day about fucking me?"

I can see he still wants to talk; I see that fight in him. But I see it slowly melting away underneath his own desire.

"Damn it, Jules," he says before he pulls me in for a long, hard kiss, our lips crashing together again like they've been starved for each other.

He hoists me up and carries me around, pushing me up against the wall while our tongues become reacquainted, laying me on the kitchen table while his fingers undo my jeans. I claw at his shirt, pulling on the cotton until it slips off of his muscles. He slips his fingers down under my panties, feeling his way into my deepest parts, controlling me like some sort of puppeteer. I drop my head back, giving him access to my neck, which his tongue trails across, driving me wild. I slide my hand down behind the waistband of his jeans and boxers, gripping him firmly in my hand and sliding it up and down until he moans.

He reaches around to unclasp my bra, throwing it to the floor, then reaches for my pants and tugs them down over my hips. When I'm completely naked, he takes a step back, his eyes feasting on me, and I feel my cheeks get hot. I tuck a piece of hair behind my ear, but he steps closer to me and reaches up, pulling it back out and letting it fall over my shoulder.

"You're beautiful, Jules," he whispers, and I feel chills ripple across my skin. He rests his forehead on mine for a moment, and I feel myself growing weak. I feel something creeping in more than just my animalistic need for him. My body wants him, but so do *I*. I want him to hold me, kiss me, talk to me, listen to me cry.

I want more.

And that's what will kill me.

I pull him in for a kiss. A long, slow, deep one. He scoops me up again and carries me up the steps to his room, laying me down gently on his bed. He stares down at me, looking right into my eyes. Our bodies are slick with sweat, and my legs open to let him in closer, but still, he holds off. He traces the side of my cheek with his thumb; he follows every outline of my face with his eyes.

I swallow beneath him.

"What...what is it?" I ask.

"I don't want…" His whispers trail off. I reach up and touch his face.

"What?"

"I don't want to *just* fuck you tonight," he whispers. I raise an eyebrow.

"Then, what do you want?"

"I want you to stay," he whispers. "And let me be whatever you need."

Yep. I'm a goner. I sigh and nod slowly, telling myself it'll just be for tonight.

He enters me swiftly, and our bodies move together like they were cut from the same

cloth. I clutch onto his, wrapping my arms around his neck and my legs around his waist. I dig my nails into his shoulders, breathing in his skin, biting his neck.

"Shane," I moan.

"Yes, baby," he whispers back, still moving on top of me. He hooks my leg over his arm, pushing himself into me further. "What do you want?"

I pause, choking on my words.

I know what I want.

I want more of this. I mean, the mindless, earth-shattering sex is great, too. But I want more of this— him holding me close to him, marking me to his memory, talking in bed, hot chocolate on the couch.

"I want you," I whisper, and to my surprise, a single tear rolls down my cheek. He holds himself off of me and uses his thumb to wipe it away.

"You have me," he whispers, bending down to kiss me one last time before we both come undone.

Going, going, gone.

26

I wake up to the sunlight beaming through the big windows at the back of his room, blinking as I slowly open my eyes. I bask in the moment: his sheets strewn around my naked body, the scent of him still lingering on my skin. But when I reach my hand backwards, he's not there.

I grab the shirt he had given me again and tug on a pair of his sweatpants before walking out into the loft. I look down over the railing, and I can hear him on the back deck. He throws his hand in the air as he talks, banging his fist down on the rail in front of him. There's anger in his voice, but all I can focus on are the muscles in his back that flex as he speaks. I pad down the steps and into the kitchen where he already has a pot of coffee made and pour myself a cup. I walk out to the living room door and tap on the glass, letting him know I'm awake. He jumps when he sees me, and I open the door slowly.

"Yeah. No, yeah. Do that. Look, I gotta go. I'll see ya in an hour," he says, clicking the end button and shoving the phone in his pocket. "Mornin'," he says as he holds his arm out toward me. I walk into him, leaning against his bare chest as the freezing air nips at my cheeks.

"Morning," I say, closing my eyes to inhale him. He tilts my chin up to him and leaves a quick kiss on my lips then smiles as he strokes my jaw with his thumb. "Everything okay?" I ask him.

"Yeah, yeah, just some shit with work," he says.

"Is it the mountain deal?" I ask. He shakes his head and rubs my arm.

"Yeah, but it's all good. Running out with Reed in a bit. It'll all be fine," he assures me before kissing my forehead. "Come on, let's go eat something."

When we get inside, he pulls out eggs and bacon from the fridge and tells me to sit at the island. I happily oblige, watching him cook while I sip on my coffee. When he's done, he flicks off the stove and turns to me with two heaping plates. I laugh as I set the coffee down and take one.

"Damn," I say, "this is enough food for teenage Shane." He laughs.

"Well, grown-up Shane will eat whatever you don't finish," he says. I smile and take a bite. "So," he says after a minute, "are we gonna talk about last night?"

I swallow the bite I'm chewing and take another sip of my coffee.

That's kind of a loaded question.

If he means, *Are we going to talk about my dad?*, then no.

If he means, *Are we going to talk about him and me and what we said?*, then still no.

I shake my head.

"There's not much to talk about," I say. He cocks his head and gives me a look.

"Jules," he says. "I won't press you on this, but your dad dying is a big deal, so whenever you're ready…"

I look up at him.

"Whenever I'm ready, what?" I ask. His eyes widen.

"I'm just saying, whenever you're ready to talk, I'll be here," he says. I put my mug down.

"Will you?"

There's a long pause, and he walks around the island and spins my stool so that we're facing each other. He leans down so that we're eye to eye, putting his hands on either side of my chair.

"If you need me, I'll be here," he says, his eyes jumping back and forth between mine, making sure I got his message. I nod slowly just as he's lowering his lips toward mine. But his phone goes off in his pocket, and he drops his head in surrender. I smile as I push up from my stool.

"I'm gonna go get dressed," I tell him as he nods and answers. I can tell that he needs to be somewhere else right now, and I don't want to put either of us in the position of him telling me that. So I put myself in it. I'm back downstairs in a moment's time, just as he's hanging up.

"I need to get into the shop today," I tell him. I awkwardly walk toward him, stepping up on my toes to kiss him gently. I look into his eyes. "Thank you for…everything."

He nods slowly.

"I'll see you tomorrow?" he asks, and I slowly turn to him with a sly smile. I nod and bite my lip.

"Tomorrow," I tell him with a wink as I get in my car and drive away.

I ACTUALLY DID HAVE to get into the shop today, although, if necessary, I could have squeezed in another morning session with Shane if time allowed. But, alas, I'm here, at the back of this little shop, putting fondant lilies on the top of another beautiful wedding cake that Marge and I started on earlier this week.

"Those look great, kid," she says as she comes around the back counter. I smile.

"Thanks," I tell her. "This is the last one, but I was going to add a few to the base, too."

She stands behind me, admiring my work.

"You have become quite the pro, haven't you?" she says with a playful nudge. I laugh.

"I learned from the best," I tell her.

"So," she says, grabbing a stool and pulling it up to the counter as I work. "How's it going with that boy back?"

I smile and shake my head.

Marge has seen Shane coming in and out of the shop to visit since he's been back. She might be older now, but she's just as sharp as ever, and nothing gets by her.

"'That boy' is fine," I tell her, trying to stay casual. "It's nice to have my old friend around."

She scoffs, and I look at her. "What?"

"'Old friends' don't drool over each other, honey," she says. I roll my eyes, even though I know it's no use lying to Marge. She always could see right through me. But I see the expression on her face grow serious as she leans forward, covering one of my hands with hers. "Listen, baby. I spoke to your mama this morning. I'm real sorry about your dad."

I swallow and nod, scratching my head. I shrug.

"I'm okay, Marge. But thank you," I say. I walk over to the sink and start washing my tools, but I feel her come up from behind me, leaning against the sink.

"Listen to me, Jules," she says, and the sternness in her voice makes me stop what I'm doing. "I know he's been gone for a while now, and I know you haven't heard a word from him since then. But this is gonna hit eventually, honey. And when it does, you make sure you let it all out."

I smile at her, her big blue eyes with so many wrinkles around them now peering into me. I nod. I picture Shane's face last night, his gentle touch as he looked down at me, imploring me to let him be who he once was to me.

You have me.

You have me, too, Shane Hunter.

"I will," I promise her. She rubs my shoulders and heads back out to the front to open up for the day.

Just as I'm putting the last of my tools away, my phone rings in my back pocket.

"Hey, Lu," I say, wiping the counters down with a rag. I hear sniffling on the other end. "Luna?" I pause.

"It went through," she whimpers, and I freeze.

"What? What did?" I ask, but I already know the answer.

"The sale. Shane's boss. He's moving forward with buying the mountain," she says, and I can hear the pain behind her voice.

"That can't be. I just talked to Shane about it this

morning. He said he was handling it with Reed, and that—"

"Ha! Reed. Reed Miller is the reason it went through," she says, and the intense pounding of my heart makes my entire body shake.

"I'll be there in a few, okay? Don't worry. We'll figure this out," I say. I hang up and untie my apron, cleaning up the kitchen and heading out to the front of the store. Marge is sitting in her chair behind the register, flipping through a magazine.

"Marge, do you mind if I run out?" I ask her. She looks at me, confused. I've never skipped out on a shift. She nods.

"Be careful, baby," she adds as I head out the door.

As soon as I get in the car, I dial his number. There's got to be some explanation, right? He seemed so sure today. But it rings and rings, going right to his voicemail. I speed down the highway and turn onto the road that leads up the mountain, past my own street and all the way to the top. I make a right at the peak and drive for a few minutes as the houses get scarcer, and all that's around are trees and land, the frozen lake below peeking through the trees. I come to the clearing where Peake's Gifts sits and pull into the empty lot.

I pull out my phone and dial him one more time before hanging up and walking inside.

I look around the store, soft Native music playing over the speakers. The store is empty, so I walk to the back room, but she's not there, either. I walk out the side door and look around till my eyes land on the dirt path that leads from the parking lot over to the ridge where we used to sit and talk about boys as teenagers. I follow it and find her, sitting on a rock, looking out over the valley.

"Haven't been back here in a while," I say as I get closer. She doesn't even turn to me; she just stares out over the water and trees, buried in winter.

"I figured I'd get in all the time up here that I can," she says, her voice riddled with sadness that shakes me. I sit down next to her and scoot in close so that our shoulders are touching.

"How's your mom?" I ask. She sighs and shrugs.

"'Bout the same as me. Feels like it's all coming to an end. Like our mark here on this mountain will be erased when all is said and done. Like it doesn't even matter." I put an arm around her shoulder and pull her into me. She rests her head on my shoulder.

"Imagine just being at peace, living on your own. Your home, your land, the essence of what makes your home just that—home. And then imagine someone coming in with a bulldozer and telling you it's theirs now."

I nod slowly. I can't imagine it. That stuff doesn't really happen to people that look like me.

"That's been happening to my people for hundreds of years. And here we are, way out into the bright future, and it's happening still," she says. It's so unlike my friend to seem so defeated. She's the tough one. She's the one who has all the answers. But right now, it looks like I need to have them.

"I'm sorry, Luna," I tell her. "But don't worry yet, okay? As soon as I talk to Shane, we will figure it all out." She nods, but I know she's not believing in anything. Her faith is gone, falling like a feather, slowly over the side of the mountain and disappearing into the valley below.

After I make sure Luna is as okay as she's going to be for now, I head back down the mountain, dialing him three more times. And each time he doesn't answer, my stomach flips.

I pull onto my street just as my phone rings, and I jump to answer it. But it's not Shane; it's Luna.

"Luna?" I answer.

"He called me," she says, her voice just above a whisper.

"Who? Shane?" I ask, my heart thudding against my chest.

"Yes," she says. "He said he was sorry. He said he did everything he could. He's going back to L.A."

There's a long pause as I stare blankly out the windshield.

"Jules?" she says.

"I'm here," I say.

"I'm sorry, Jules," she mutters. I shake my head.

"No, Luna, *I'm* sorry," I say. "I can't believe this is happening to you."

"I know," she says. "But I can't believe it's happening to you again, either. After all you've been through."

But as I turn into my driveway and see his rental car parked, I hit the brakes. I look up and see him sitting on my porch, his face somber and scared.

"Gotta go, Lu," I tell her. "Love you."

I get out of the car slowly, holding myself steady. I close the door and glare at him, then I take a breath and walk toward him. I feel my hands shaking with equal parts fear and anger. He stands as I approach, but I walk past him to the door, opening it and dropping my stuff inside before closing it again.

He's not coming in this house.

"Jules, I—"

"Just tell me it's not true," I say, cutting him off. His eyes are wide. "Tell me Reed Miller is not selling the mountain to your boss."

He shakes his head slowly, biting his bottom lip and dropping his head. I close my eyes for a moment.

This is it.

"Jules, I tried—"

"It's my turn to talk," I say, holding a hand up, and he snaps his mouth shut. I walk past him toward the porch railing, looking out into the woods as I gather my thoughts. Then, I turn back to him.

"Not even twelve hours ago, you told me things were under control with the sale. You told me it was fine. And then—what's worse—you looked me in the eye and said, 'If you need me, I'll be there.' Do you remember that?" I ask. He nods, unsure if it's rhetorical or not.

"Jules—"

I hold my hand up again.

"It's one thing to fuck me over, but it's a completely separate thing to do it to Luna. Or to the other people in this town. This was your *home*. You might have left for bigger and better, but for the rest of us, this is as big and better as it's going to get. And you'll just leave us with whatever destruction you cause on your way back out."

I'm seething, the anger hot on my lips as I speak. I drop my head and shake it, so disappointed in where I've let myself go.

"The worst part about all of this, though, is that I did the one thing I swore I would never do again. I let you look me in the eye and tell me I meant something. I let you in my bed, and I got in yours, knowing all the while there was a good chance you'd up and leave again. I guess at least this time you had the decency to say goodbye."

He narrows his eyes, his chest rising and falling with heavy breaths as he shakes his head.

"Jules, that's not—"

"Enough, Shane. It's my turn now. Go, so that I can start this whole process over again. And do me a favor. Don't come back in eleven more years. I won't be waiting," I say before opening the door and stepping inside.

27

It's been a few days, and I'm trying like hell to remember how long I felt like a train had hit me after he left the first time. I wake up on my couch, my tear-stained pillow beneath my head, the blanket I had pulled from the top of the couch lying over me. I remember everything slowly: Luna, Shane, the deal. Me telling him to leave and not come back.

I run into town and grab coffees and an assortment of donuts, then I head back up the mountain. Luna and I will both be grieving today, and the best way to get through grief is by eating a ton of sugar. Everyone knows that.

We sit on the edge of the counter, quietly sipping and munching as we both stare off into space. Luna's afraid her past will be wiped from memory. I'm afraid I'll never be able to forget mine.

"Did you talk to him?" she asks between bites. I nod.

"Yeah," I say. "It didn't go well."

"What happened?"

"Well, for starters, he didn't deny that Reed was

selling the land to his boss," I say. She nods. "So I told him to go."

"Damn, Jules, I'm sorry," she says, shaking her head. "I thought he was different."

I laugh.

"You and me both," I tell her.

We both pause when we hear a man's voice coming from outside, talking loudly and laughing. We jump up off the counter and walk to the front door.

Reed Fucking Miller.

Just standing in the parking lot, his dress shoes sinking into the mud left by last week's snowstorm. But he doesn't seem to care. He's talking into his phone like he's the only fucking person up here on this mountain. Without hesitating, Luna bursts out of the front door, making a beeline for him. I follow closely behind, more for Reed's sake than for Luna's.

"Something funny?" she asks as she gets closer, crossing her arms over her chest and glaring at him with a look that I'm pretty sure could blast holes through his skull. He looks from her to me, then back to her.

"Hey, Rod, let me give you a call back. Yeah, mhmm, sounds good. Talk soon," he says, hanging up. "Morning, ladies. I'm—"

"I know who the fuck you are, Reed," Luna says. I swallow. Poor Reed doesn't know what he's in for. He tucks his outstretched hand back into his coat pocket.

"Have we met?" he asks with a questioning look.

"No. But you went ahead and sold my mountain," she says. "I'm Luna Peake, and you've just become my worst fucking enemy."

He stands back, nodding slowly, trying to fit the pieces together.

"What are you doing up here?" she asks impatiently. "The sale hasn't gone through yet. And even when it does, *I* own this part of the mountain."

"Peake," he says, looking beyond us at the Peake's Gifts sign above the store. "I see. I, uh, was just doing a little survey of the land for my client. Sorry, it seems like we got off on the wrong foot," he says.

She rolls her eyes, her jaw twitching back and forth as she looks him up and down.

"There will be no righting this wrong, Miller," she says before turning on her foot and walking back into the shop. We stand awkwardly for a moment before I go to follow her, but he speaks.

"Peake," he says again. "Her family are the ones who…"

I nod, watching as he figures it out.

"She's the one who was friends with Shane Hunter," he says. My eyes widen at just the mention of his name.

"*Was*," I say, making that very, *very* clear. He nods.

"You know Shane?" he asks. I nod slowly.

"I used to."

"Man, poor guy. He tried so hard to find another spot for his boss," he says. "Up until yesterday, we thought he had. There's this spot a few miles outside of town, twice the acreage of the mountain. Shane thought he had it in the bag, even had the contracts written up for Rod. But at the last minute, Rod changed his mind."

He turns to walk toward his truck, squeaky clean with big, shiny wheels. Definitely not a truck that belongs to a Meade Lake resident.

"He must really care about you all," Reed says before he gets in, and our eyes meet.

"Why do you say that?"

"He got passed over for that promotion because he refused to be a part of the mountain sale. Looks like his boss is making him go back to the L.A. office. He's a good dude. I'll miss him around here. Well, take care."

I watch as Reed Miller peels away in the snow and ice, leaving me completely shaken and not even knowing it.

I STAND in the parking lot for a minute, the cold air blowing all around me, my hair flying in wisps in front of my face.

He refused to be a part of the mountain sale.

He wasn't leaving me again. He didn't break our hearts or our trust. He tried to save them, to the point of him passing up a promotion.

He did it for us.

For me.

I get in my car and put the key in the ignition, speeding back down the mountain toward my house. I know what I have to do, and I know where I'm going. I'm packing a bag, stopping at his mother's to find out where he lives, and then I'm flying to L.A.

But when I pull into the driveway, I slam on the brakes again, the sight of him on my porch like a painfully beautiful deja vu. He stands as soon as I get out, and I walk toward him slowly, not sure if it's real or not.

I walk up the steps and face him so we're just a foot or two apart.

"Hi," I say quietly, my eyes jumping back and forth to his.

"Jules, I need to say something, okay?" he says. I

nod. He draws in a long breath and blows it out. "I once told you that if someone didn't fight to keep you in their life, they didn't deserve you."

I nod slowly.

"I remember," I tell him. It was the year anniversary of my dad leaving.

"Well, Jules, here I am," he says, holding his arms out. "I'm fighting for you. I'll take all the time you need. I'll do whatever you want me to do. I'll be your friend— and not the kind that sleeps with you—if that's what you want. However you'll have me in your life, that's what I'll do, Jules. Because I'd rather have you like that than not have you at all."

Tears well in my eyes as he stands, breathless, waiting for me to respond.

Finally, I take a few steps toward him and press up to kiss his lips.

"I love you, Hunter," I whisper when we come apart. "Does that answer the question of how I want you in my life?"

He smiles down at me, tucking a copper lock behind my ear.

"I've always loved you, Grey," he says.

I think back to when we were kids, spending our days with our friends, not a care in the world. I go back to winters past, all those nights out on the ice and snow. I held him at bay, afraid I'd lose him. And then I lost him anyway.

But he came back, just like he did that night on the ice. He threw me a lifeline that night. But I realize now that we'd been throwing each other lifelines for our whole friendship. We pulled each other out of the darkness so many times; we were each other's warmth when the cold became too much.

I know it won't always be pretty. I know there will be more dark times, as there always are. But we can handle the ugly together. Because even the darkest winter nights melt into the brightest days.

EPILOGUE

I lean back on my hands, letting the warm breeze blow through my hair as I squeeze the sand between my fingers. I close my eyes and listen to the seagulls squawking above, the sounds of the people on the Ferris wheel laughing and screaming in the background.

"Fries for the lady," Shane says as he hands me my container, sitting down next to me in the sand. This is the first time I've ever seen the Pacific Ocean, and I can't help but smile.

"What?" he says.

"I was just thinking about how I always imagined the first time I'd come out to California would be with you," I say. "And here we are." He smiles and leans in for a salty kiss between fries. He quit his job before we left Meade Lake, and we flew in a few days ago to pack up his apartment and get his car. We will drive back to Meade Lake at the end of the week, and I still can't believe he's coming back for good.

"It's beautiful out here, huh?" he asks. I nod, looking

around. It really is. Everything here seems to be in this peaceful, bright haze.

"It is," I agree, looking back out over the water. "Was living here everything you thought it would be?"

He claps the salt off his hands and looks around.

Then he shakes his head.

"Living here was a dream," he says. "Beautiful weather, beautiful people. But it never felt quite right. And it's because I didn't want to come to California. Not really."

I look at him inquisitively.

"I wanted to come to California with *you*," he says. "You were what I wanted. I wanted to be wherever you were."

"Well, then," I tell him as I push him down into the sand and climb on top of him, "let's go home."

THE MEADE LAKE SERIES

Did you enjoy In Winters Past?

Read the other books in the Meade Lake series!

Back to Shore, Mila and Ryder's story

Stones Unturned, Derrick and Kaylee's story

ACKNOWLEDGMENTS

HUGE thank you to my family for dealing with me clicking away at my keyboard getting this story down. Dani & team, I cannot thank you enough for going back and forth a million and one times before landing on everything that we did for this series.

Kimbo, thank you for reading every word I write, for loving romance as much as me, and for all your help with all things swimming.

To my beautiful author friends who are constantly offering me advice, a listening ear, a shoulder to virtually cry on, or a good *Schitt's Creek* meme, I would truly be lost without you.

ABOUT TAYLOR

T.D. Colbert is a romance and women's fiction author. When she's not chasing her kids or hanging with her husband, she's probably under her favorite blanket, either reading a book or writing one. She lives in Maryland, where she was born and raised. For more information, visit www.taylordanaecolbert.com.

Follow T.D. on TikTok, Instagram and Twitter, @taydanaewrites, and on Facebook, Author T.D. Colbert, for information on upcoming books!

Are you a blogger or a reader who wants in on some secret stuff? Sign up for my newsletter, and join **TDC's VIPs** - T.D.'s reader group on Facebook for exclusive information on her next books, early cover reveals, giveaways, and more!

OTHER BOOKS BY T.D. COLBERT:

T.D. Colbert's Author Page

NOTE FROM THE AUTHOR

Dear Reader,

I can't tell you what it means that you've decided, out of all of the books in all the world, to read mine.

If you enjoyed reading it as much as I enjoyed writing it, please consider leaving an Amazon or GoodReads review (or both!). Reviews are crucial to a book's success, and I can't thank you enough for leaving one (or a few!)!

Thank you for taking the time to read *Stones Unturned*.

Always,
    TDC
    www.tdcolbert.com
    @taydanaewrites